»»»» ‹‹«««
The Town *of N*

»»»»»»»»»»»»»»»«««««««««««««««

Leonid Dobychin

The Town of N

TRANSLATED FROM THE RUSSIAN BY
RICHARD C. BORDEN WITH
NATALIA BELOVA

INTRODUCTION BY
RICHARD C. BORDEN

NORTHWESTERN UNIVERSITY PRESS

EVANSTON, ILLINOIS

»»»»»»»»»»»»»»»»«««««««««««««««

Northwestern University Press
Evanston, Illinois 60208-4210

Copyright © 1998 by Northwestern University Press. Published 1998.
All rights reserved.

Printed in the United States of America

ISBN 0-8101-1589-1

Library of Congress Cataloging-in-Publication Data

Dobychin, Leonid.
    [Gorod Ėn. English]
    The town of N / Leonid Dobychin ; translated from
the Russian by Richard C. Borden with Natalia Belova ;
introduction by Richard C. Borden.
        p. cm. — (European classics)
    ISBN 0-8101-1589-1
    I. Borden, Richard C. (Richard Chandler) II. Belova, Natalia.
III. Title. IV. Series: European classics (Evanston, Ill.)
PG3476.D573G6713 1998
891.73'42—dc21   98-15528
                                                            CIP

»»» CONTENTS «««

Leonid Dobychin's *The Town of N:* Introduction

Leonid Dobychin (1894–1936) was one of the most tragic figures in a Russian literary history replete with tragedies and unnatural deaths. Dobychin was a nervous, awkward, and proud man who lived a lonely life and died a lonelier death. Likened to brilliant eccentrics such as Velimir Khlebnikov, Paul Gauguin, and Bruno Schulz, he worked for most of his adult life as a poorly paid statistician in a provincial town, occupying a single room with four relatives, none of whom offered anything but scorn for his literary aspirations. He did not even have his own table at which to write until, at the age of forty, he received a room in a Leningrad communal apartment from the Writers' Union. He was destined to disappear less than two years later, an apparent suicide.[1]

Dobychin was one of the truly original and gifted writers of his day. Nevertheless, his only novel, *The Town of N,* for all practical purposes vanished together with its author following its publication in 1935. After more than a half-century, it has been rediscovered, and is now recognized as a masterpiece of world literature.

It is, however, perhaps misleading to speak of Dobychin's "rediscovery," for, despite the high regard in which Yury Tynyanov, Kornei Chukovsky, Veniamin Kaverin, Evgeny Shvarts, and other leading writers of the day held his work, Dobychin was scarcely discovered in the first place. His known oeuvre, until the appearance of previously unpublished stories in the 1990s, consisted of two slim collections, which appeared in 1927 and 1931, and *The Town of N*, first published in Moscow in an edition of 7,200. The complexity of the short stories, their lack of anything resembling conventional plots, and their darkly satirical view of the new Soviet society all guaranteed that they, at least, would remain obscure among the reading public at large. And before the much more accessible *Town of N* could find its deserved audience, both the book and its author had long vanished.

Soviet critics were predictably rough on Dobychin's novel when it first appeared, attacking it principally for its "formalist" style at a time when "formalism" was, in the eyes of the state, ideologically anathema. Critics also noted that this formalism was grafted onto a negative, naturalistic, even "decadent" view of humanity. It is, in fact, something of a mystery how the book was published at all at the height of Stalinism, when dogmatic conservatism, to say nothing of philistinism, ruled the art establishment. *The Town of N*, by some distance, represents the last seed of Russian literary avant-gardism to have sprouted within the Soviet Union until at least the 1960s. It is a unique, utterly original creation, perhaps the last truly subtle work of art to appear in Russia for a full fifty years. Critics took the view—quite correctly, in fact—that by linking Gogol's provincial Russia at the beginning of the nineteenth century with the Russia portrayed in *The Town of N* a century later, and by showing how little had changed in social and human nature, Dobychin implicitly articulated a deep skepticism regarding the official Marxist understanding of humanity's and society's inescapable advance through historical processes. This contention was supported by the fact that Dobychin's stories, published earlier, at a time of considerably more freedom, had portrayed an "N" that was explicitly Soviet, wherein the new system and ideology had created nothing but a new coloration for the same essential bleakness. For its stylistic originality and its naturalistic worldview, *The Town of N* was more than once described by its critics as "Joycean," which, of course, was meant as opprobrium, something on the order of "bourgeois decadent," but which has become from today's perspective rich, and richly deserved, praise.

On January 28, 1936, a few months after *The Town of N*'s publication, the infamous *Pravda* attack on the composer Shostakovich's modernistic music initiated a savage campaign against "formalism" in all the arts. At a meeting of the Leningrad Writers' Union that convened shortly thereafter, Dobychin was singled out as the first "whipping boy"—the "chief formalist"—among Leningrad writers. Anticipating the Sinyavsky-Daniel trial of 1966, Dobychin's critics accused him, absurdly, of sharing his fictional characters' views, notably those of his child protagonist in *The Town of N*, whose nearsighted vision of society was cast as a reflection of Dobychin's own political nearsightedness. Dobychin was appalled at this willful misreading of his book and at the unsubtle hints of some speakers about his being a class enemy. He responded only by stating that, regrettably, he could not agree with what had been said, and departed. He disappeared the next day, after organizing his affairs and confiding plans to kill himself to an acquaintance, who later proved to have been the police spy assigned to report on his activities. He was never seen again.

Veniamin Kaverin writes in his memoirs that Dobychin's death should be regarded as murder plain and simple. He also hypothesizes that Dobychin's suicide was an act of "self-affirmation." Dobychin considered his novel a work of Europe-wide significance, and killing himself, like a Japanese commiting hara-kiri, was intended as an emblem of his contempt for those involved in his supposed "disgrace."[2]

Dobychin's return to the public domain during the period of Gorbachev's policy of "openness" began in 1987, with the republication of some of his stories. A volume containing all of the works published in the 1920s and 1930s appeared in 1989 in the series "The Forgotten Book," and during the 1990s several of Dobychin's previously unpublished stories have appeared in journals. Dobychin may well prove to have been the single most significant revelation in Russian letters during glasnost, at least for those among the Russian cultural elite and in the West who had long been familiar with writers such as Solzhenitsyn, Nabokov, Shalamov, and Platonov who had been banned in the Soviet Union. In fact, Dobychin's influence is already being felt. In a recent essay by one of Russia's leading writers and critics, Dobychin was listed, along with Nabokov, Borges, and Pound, among the "previously unknown" writers who are influencing the "alternative" stream in Russian prose fiction today.[3]

The Town of N is set among the early twentieth-century Russian middle classes of an unidentified Latvian city. While this city is recognizable as Daugavpils, formerly Dvinsk, Dobychin's home for much of his life, the reader understands by the novel's title, taken from Nikolai Gogol's satirical classic *Dead Souls,* that this is at least partially a symbolic space—an Everyplace, or at least a representative provincial Russian milieu, one that is by definition far from ideal. Like Gogol's "N," Dobychin's town defines something of a "fallen" world, a spiritual wasteland that seems to offer little promise of redemption, populated as it is by citizens who are smug, hypocritical, bigoted, and often mean. Through his title, Dobychin suggests that his characters are the latter-day counterparts to Gogol's cast of rogues and buffoons: the con man Chichikov, the insipid Manilov, the miser Plyushkin, Sobakevich the misanthrope, Nozdryov the liar. This fact may not be obvious at first to Dobychin's readers, for his characters are neither typical nor satirically conceived, and because the novel is narrated by a little boy who accepts as fact everything presented to him by adults. Thus, for much of the novel, he does not perceive the deep flaws in the principals of his universe, just as he fails, upon first reading *Dead Souls,* to recognize that Gogol's characters are comic cartoons, not meant to be taken, as he believes, as models for emulation.

By the time Gogol had finished the first volume of his epic "poem"—what we know today as *Dead Souls*—he had conceived of one, and perhaps two additional volumes, somewhat along the lines of Dante's *Divine Comedy,* with its "Inferno," "Purgatorio," and "Paradisio." These were to have concluded with the rogue hero Chichikov's spiritual regeneration, as well as, by implication, that of all Russia itself. Gogol struggled for the next decade to complete the second volume, but burned the manuscript shortly before his death. His "N," therefore, remains mired forever in that unregenerate state, the "inferno," so to speak, defining Chichikov's adventures in volume 1. So, too, by implication, does Dobychin's N.

The Town of N in part falls within the boundaries of the literary "childhood": it is told with poignant unreliability from the perspective of a nameless boy. The "childhood" is an important Russian tradition, which encompasses works by writers from Tolstoy, Goncharov, and Aksakov to Gorky, Bely, and Nabokov.[4] But, unlike the more traditional line in Russian childhood fiction, which imagines the experience of childhood as a nearly ideal state, a figurative garden, Dobychin's "childhood" is almost gardenless. Or, perhaps, it portrays a garden defined as much by the snake that also occupies paradise as by its traditional idyll. In this sense, *The Town of N* recalls Ivan Goncharov's vision of childhood in *Oblomov,* where an aura of decay and corruption permeates "paradise." Given that *The Town of N* was written under the straitened circumstances that obtained in Stalinist Russia, it is also important not to ignore the "anti-childhood" tradition that became fashionable in Soviet literature, when the state required of its artists that the prerevolutionary world in which they grew up be portrayed in less than positive terms. It is not impossible that Dobychin's jaundiced representation of a provincial, prerevolutionary Russian childhood was at least partly influenced by such considerations, reflecting an attempt to follow in its social and political orientation officially authorized conceptions of prerevolutionary childhood, which exposed the cruel environment that was to produce Russia's revolutionaries—or at least the Revolution's sympathizers—and for which Maxim Gorky's biographical *Childhood* served as the paradigm.

Of course, in most ways Dobychin's "childhood" resembles no other. *The Town of N* distinguishes itself radically from even the best Soviet "anti-childhoods" in its complexity, its irony, and its absence of overt tendentiousness. Dobychin leaves all conclusions about the society he portrays to the skills of good readers, who absorb telling detail through the narrative's ironic veil and its faux neutrality in representing characters' actions and words.

Another literary context to which Dobychin's writing bears some kinship is the avant-garde "Oberiu" ("Association for Real Art") group, which was active in Leningrad from 1927 to 1930, and included irreverent, iconoclastic absurdists and comic satirists such as Daniil Kharms and Aleksandr Vvedensky. Others whose works share some of Dobychin's experimental poetics and darkly comic worldview are such masters of satire and the syntax of the absurd as Andrei Platonov and Mikhail Zoshchenko. But Dobychin by nature was incapable of joining any school or grouping. While among his contemporaries he singled out Zoshchenko and Tynyanov for (not unqualified) praise, he was a generally severe and cutting judge of his fellow writers' efforts. He himself claimed to pay little heed to criticism, which he considered pointless in his case since he had no intention or capacity to write other than as he did. That he never belonged to any of the influential arts circles then in fashion, however, at least partly explains why his memory was never properly engraved into the era's cultural history.

The Town of N is based on autobiographical and historical fact. Dobychin scholars have identified real-life models for many of the novel's characters and institutions.[5] Dobychin's own father, like his character's, was a doctor who died when the future writer was still a child. His mother was a midwife, a profession Dobychin transfers to the child's mother's friend, A. L. A certain "Zachs" really did own the local match factory, where the city's first revolutionary activity took place. There really was an important 1905 incident in Dvinsk, following Russia's ignominious defeat at the hands of Japan and the bloody uprisings in Petersburg and Riga. Demonstrators were shot upon as they marched down the city's main street. This precipitated further turmoil when twenty thousand citizens accompanied the deceased to the cemetery—a scene reconstructed in *The Town of N* when Vasya Strizhkin is shot in the buttocks, and demonstrators march past the child's windows for so long that he and his mother supposedly lose all interest. The flurry of church building and religious discussion portrayed in chapter 18 was spurred by the newly won freedom of conscience, one of the rights conferred upon Russia's citizens after the events of 1905. There really was a "Siou & Co., Moscow"; its cookie tins have become collectors' items. The Strauss family really made sausages. Even the play that the child spies Sophie Samokvasova and Alexander Lieberman rehearsing apparently really exists.[6] Other events marked in *The Town of N,* ranging from the death of Tolstoy to the transference of the holy relics of Efrosinia of Polotsk and the centennial celebrations of Gogol's birth, were all important dates on the local and national calendars, and serve as the lone markers—along with changes of season, celebrations of feast days, and beginnings and endings of school years—of time's passage in the novel. Most important, it is not difficult to perceive in the child narrator

Dobychin's comic self-portrait: the future writer's blundering path toward a unique vision of the world; the "Portrait of the Artist as a Young Fool"; the lonely little boy suddenly recognized as a "poet."

In Dobychin's novel childhood innocence rarely goes beyond ignorance, comic naïveté, and misperception. The worm of social corruption has burrowed within the child's apprehension of his world, and his child's defamiliarizing assimilation of experience carries pollution from the world of adults. The child himself, of course, is by no means bad. He is, in fact, the unique token of beauty and grace in his universe. But his is a beauty for which others always seem to be grasping. And they grasp with much the same desperation and potential destructiveness that is directed at the child's closest literary forebear, Sasha Pylnikov, the fallen angel of Fyodor Sologub's symbolist-satirical *A Petty Demon*. We with whom Dobychin's hero shares his thoughts understand through comic recognition that his vision, both figurative and literal, is skewed, and that he will have to overcome everything he will learn in his childhood if he and his world are to be redeemed.

On the surface, *The Town of N*'s narrative comprises a slight, diffuse selection of the detail constituting a child's small world, beginning when he is seven years old in 1901 and concluding ten years later. In a telegraphic, often humorous staccato ("Snow covered the cobblestones. It grew still. We sacked Cecilia."), with comic misunderstanding and the sketchiest figurations of character and event, the child evokes his universe—its shops, its churches belonging to five different faiths and as many ethnic groups, its concomitant prejudice, its marriages, betrayals, lottery winners, new technologies, and sexual mysteries. Like a miniature *Ulysses*, *The Town of N* introduces more than one hundred characters in barely that many pages. Often these characters are identified by a single trait or deed. They appear, disappear, and reappear in cameos, most never acquiring a third dimension, but somehow getting their stories told.

There is Madame Strauss, wife of the local sausage maker, who is in love with Kapellmeister Schmidt, and fated to be killed by the copper ham that hangs above the sausage shop door. There is "Madmazelle" Gorshkova, teacher of foreign languages, who swells and slows as the years advance, but whose emotional gusts and clutches the child still must vigilantly plot to avoid.

No line of thought, image, or event in Dobychin's novel is painted with more than a few dexterous strokes. The narrative remains oblique in its thematic concerns. Authorial editorialization is confined to ironic implication and understatement. As in Dobychin's brilliant short stories, there is nothing even remotely akin to a plot, but rather a sort of arbitrary chronology that carries us from season to season. Nevertheless, *The Town of N* weaves a complex and vivid tapestry of prerevolutionary provincial society, a place little farther along the road to redemption than its namesake of a century before.

Dobychin's texts demand close reading and rereading. Much information necessary for appreciating their subtleties is revealed nonsequentially and inexplicitly. But rereadings bear large rewards. What at first appears to be random detail—little arbitrary dabs of color—when seen from a perspective of familiarity and distance (the comparison with pointillism in the plastic arts is apt) join together in patterns to create a complex and harmonious panorama. Details become linked within a network of associative sense, a fabric of meaning comprising interactive thematic threads or axes, themselves devised from interacting motifs. These thematic axes include: the quest for ideal friendship; betrayal; vengeance; sexual predation and repression; civil and religious rebellion and repression; expulsion from paradise; resurrection; and the remembering of childhood. Recurring motifs include funerals, punishments, falling, "progress," angels, floggings, beards, gilt, eavesdropping, foreign-language instruction, the life of Jesus, the Mother of God, and Nietzsche.

To delineate *The Town of N*'s mechanics of meaning in accessible terms, it is probably necessary to extract these individual threads from their matrices, though to do so reduces the novel's textural richness, which springs from the multiform ways—thematic, structural, parodic—in which these threads collide with and shape one another. For purposes of introduction, however, one might follow the thread that links motifs belonging to the themes of sexual repression and predation. As mediated by the child's tendency to equate physical resemblance with essence, this thread would connect his childhood sweetheart, Nathalie, to a scene from a play rehearsal (which seems to involve Alexander Pushkin and his wife, Natalya) he had once caught a glimpse of, in which a young woman on her knees begs forgiveness of a man she calls Alexander (played by another Alexander, Lieberman), who remains unmoved by her entreaties. It also links up in the child's mind with Mary Magdalene, as she is depicted in a painting of the biblical passage known as "Noli me tangere," which the child has seen on Easter postcards. "Noli me tangere," an important figure within Christian iconography, originates in John 20:17, where Christ admonishes Mary Magdalene not to touch him as he rises from the tomb. It has been the subject of innumerable paintings in Western art, one of which the child describes: "a striking woman kneeled before a naked Jesus Christ, who had a sheet thrown over him, and her arms reached out to him" (chapter 24). This, of course, is essentially the same image as that created by the real-life Sophie Samokvasova and Alexander Lieberman, as that enacted by the play characters Natalya Goncharova and Alexander Pushkin, and as that imagined by the child when he pictures himself and Nathalie together. The child does not know until much later, when he briefly studies Latin, that "Noli me tangere" means "Don't touch me." But the picture's iconography, it seems, fits his needs.

A continuous threat, at least as perceived by the child, arises from the enigmatic spheres of sexuality and physical intimacy. He is assailed by what he regards as predations of all sorts from nearly everyone, from his neighbor's housekeeper to his father confessor. One semiconscious response to such threats is perhaps inspired by the "Noli me tangere" motif, by the examples of Christ and the two Alexanders, Pushkin and Lieberman, who when assailed by apparently grasping women simply stand their ground and say "Noli me tangere!" Another response to sexual threats comes in the child's mentally casting a schoolmate as his avenging angel.

A second thread, thus, follows Vasya Strizhkin, an older schoolboy who is famous for having been flogged, who later becomes a policeman and, despite never formally meeting the hero (except when, in a crowd, he gives him an anonymous fillip on the back of the head), absurdly comes to represent in the child's imagination a guardian angel, as well as a fallen angel, an avenging angel, a Christ figure, a beloved disciple, and an admired representative of official repression. This Vasya, thus, represents in the child's confused mind both the angel and the cop of his universe, the spiritual and corporeal delegate of church and state. He is both martyr and torturer. That this is all so mixed up in the child's head perhaps illustrates the fallen state of N, and of the institutions to which its citizens pay obeisance. The only hope implicitly offered in Dobychin's N is art itself, that the child may become the Raphael or Leonardo da Vinci who can uplift with beauty, or the latter-day Gogol who will hold a mirror up to N so that its denizens may see themselves for whom they truly are—descendants of Chichikov and Manilov, Sobakevich and Nozdryov.

As these and the many other thematic threads indicate, *The Town of N,* like many "childhood" narratives, on one level operates epistemologically, exploring the question of what the child knows and how he knows it. His acquisition of knowledge proves arduous, a ten-year misadventure of false leads and dead ends. The child is rarely certain of what is and what is not, a fact reflected in the text by his frequently reporting, verbatim, others' opinions and pronouncements as if they were his own, and by his often assuming an identity of "we" to report his involvement in events he does not fully understand, or for which he is disinclined to assume responsibility. It is also marked by the child's habit of using quotation marks to indicate things, the exact nature of which he is unsure.

One epistemological tool for Dobychin's child is literature. *The Town of N* is an intensely "literary" work. In its "literariness" it recalls the writing of James Joyce, whose stories in *Dubliners* come as close as anything to resembling Dobychin's art, especially in their creation in miniature of an entire urban organism, with its social, religious, political, and cultural dimensions all evoked with the minimum of deft strokes. Literariness and irony are, in fact, *The Town of N*'s defining traits.

The child uses the books he reads as prisms through which he views and struggles to comprehend his world. He seeks in books not merely answers to questions that trouble him, but topics for conversation, models of behavior, and comic material to attract companions. When he longs for ideal friendship, he imagines it to arrive literally in the persons of Alyosha Karamazov, Prince Myshkin, or the "Adolescent"—all young characters from the novels of Dostoevsky. When he drops his friendship with a boy named Schuster, it is because that boy does not read enough, and therefore the child finds it difficult to converse with him. This comical, touching reliance on books to tell one how to live engenders light-hearted satire of all those famous figures in the Russian novel—from Pushkin's Tatyana and Onegin to Dostoevsky's Underground Man—whose behavior is shaped by the books they read.

Running along these same lines is a *Don Quixote* subtext, introduced when the child's new friend, Serge, shows him that novel and sums up its contents with a succinct, "He was a fool." Of course, the child narrator, unlike this pragmatic friend, is also a "fool" by the same definition. Like Quixote, Dobychin's child consistently mis-sees his world, and does so until a final revelation (in the child's case, through the acquisition of eyeglasses). Also like Quixote, Dobychin's child is blinded by romantic notions drawn from novels, and hobbled by a failure to recognize that the rules operating in fiction do not necessarily apply to life.

The Town of N is also rich in pocket-sized parodies, such as that involving the local Anna Karenina, Olga Kuskova, a young woman who lets herself be run over by a train when Serge's mother puts a stop to her illicit romance with that teenaged boy. The most significant subtext among many, however, may be Sologub's *A Petty Demon*, whose themes and details Dobychin parodies on virtually every page of his novel.

The primary texts from which the child extrapolates understanding of his world are *Dead Souls* and "The Sacred Story" (with Tolstoy, Chekhov, Dickens, and others figuring in his later development). Unfortunately, as a reader he proves to be a comic failure. His reading of *Dead Souls,* for example, shapes his aspirations for ideal friendship, which he perceives in the relationship between Manilov and Chichikov. His readings are senseless to irony, satire, or parody. And so he dreams of going to Gogol's N, where, like Chichikov, he "would be loved." He dreams of friendship with Manilov's sons, Alcides and Themistoclius. He imagines that he and his new acquaintance Serge, like Chichikov and Manilov, will aspire to live and study sciences together. He never understands that N is where he already lives.

This basic misunderstanding provides the paradigm that obtains throughout the novel, as the child ever pursues the ideal, while continually bumping up against the real. It is a dichotomy that parodically reflects a symbolist's, such as Sologub's, aspirations for an Otherworld, an ideal that exists somewhere beyond this fallen state.

The "ideal" to which the child first aspires, Gogol's N, reflects a ludicrous misreading of Gogol's text, and the child's disillusionment is inevitable, just as it will be in all his subsequent pursuits of love, truth, and beauty. Vasya the angel becomes a cop. The Magdalene's loving reach becomes a sexual threat. "Love, truth and beauty!"—the theme of a teacher's speech at the child's graduation ceremonies, just before the novel's conclusion—can only ring with hollow irony for the nearly grown boy; by now he has long abandoned such ideals and, as he prepares to set off upon life's journey, is thereby armed against illusion and the traps it can spring. He will see and "read" the world clearly now, as it really is, as he himself has finally seen it. He now knows that the only "Paradise for Children" in his N is the toy shop of that name. Now he will see for the first time and forever after the actual stars in the actual sky, not just those pictures of stars on the church ceiling he had studied as a child.

The second method by which Dobychin's child will create his early understanding of his world is by studying the resemblance the people and things around him bear to pictures he has seen, be they famous paintings, book illustrations, or advertisements in shop windows. He then, mistakenly of course, posits essential similarities where he has perceived formal ones. In fact, pointillistic would also be a good description for the child's perception and gradual cognition of his world. He has, up close, no perspective, no objective point of observation from which to assimilate the details he encounters. Thus he can neither literally nor metaphorically see the big picture, the fact that he lives in a virtual inversion of that ideal toward which he aspires. Or, to borrow another metaphor, the child observes his world much as the midwife A. L. teaches the child and his mother to examine paintings—"through the fist": with the surroundings blocked out, with a sort of blinkered vision, reducing the world to a succession of discrete snapshots. The child's early attempts at cognition through such comparisons are drawn, of course, from a limited fund of things already known and named in his world, and they often humorously fail to convey an object's essence. The child, for example, identifies his mother's new friend as resembling the illustration of "Chichikov" in his copy of *Dead Souls*. She thus becomes "the lady Chichikov."

Similar to the process by which myth originates among primitive peoples, Dobychin's child uses his tools of metaphor to create stories that help him explain the world around him and to protect himself against its threats. He is a sort of mythmaker, a spinner of fairy tales. And these fairy tales seem to comfort him, to offer, if only subconsciously, possible solutions to difficulties, answers to mysteries, a promise of hope. Principal agents in the child's mythopoetics, as we have seen, are people such as Vasya Strizhkin and pictures such as "Noli me tangere," the "Sistine Madonna," and "The Last Supper." The fatal flaw in the child's epistemology here, however, is that, just as he proved to be a bad reader of texts, so he has very poor eyesight, something he does not fully appreciate until the end of the novel. Thus, much of what he "sees" is wrong. This includes many "resemblances" that simply are not there. He also makes aesthetic judgments that might not bear the scrutiny of the better-sighted, as he himself eventually begins to suspect. Even accepting the validity of this improbable method of epistemology, therefore, the end product in this instance would be suspect. Both physically and figuratively the child "sees" Vasya Strizhkins who do not exist, misreads friendly gestures as threatening assaults, and admires beautiful Nathalies who may not look at all as he believes.

When readers reach the novel's conclusion and learn, in a comic "laying bare" of the novel's central metaphor, that the newly bespectacled child has all his life been mis-seeing his world, they must return, like the child himself, to the very beginning and once again examine and evaluate each detail anew. This time, both will benefit from a clearer vision and the healthy perspective of comic skepticism.

Dobychin was an excrutiatingly slow writer who would spend days, even months, on the tiniest of details, often producing stories of but four or five pages in length and expressing astonishment, perhaps disingenuously, that others could churn out so many works of dimensions attractive to publishers. The result of such laborious creation is that the reader may invest fully in each detail—each word, each oddity of syntax, diction, or style—confident that it has been selected for its maximum informativeness. Nothing has been left to chance.

The idiosyncrasies of Dobychin's style render certain of his narrative subtleties difficult to translate. The reader of the original Russian often feels off balance. Dobychin's diction at times sounds pretentious and artificial ("bitter for me this was"). Few sentences follow conventional literary syntax. Punctuation can be bizarre. None of this, however, exists for its own sake. Part of the verbal juggling act reflects the author's ironic exposition of his narrator's perception and cognition of his world.[7] It represents the author winking at his readers from over his character's shoulder, revealing the child's naïveté and comic misunderstanding, his assumption of adult poses and pretensions. This humorous disclosure of character and authorial stance is achieved variously, by means of mismatched comparisons, for example, or incongruous juxtapositions ("And he told how he flogs him in the presence of the police: at home the swine bawls and the neighbors come running. I would then remember Vasya. Childhood's poetry would revive in me."), rhetorical deflations of expectation ("If Nathalie were suddenly to appear here . . . —I would say to her: —Hello."), and absurd understatement (of a young woman who has committed suicide, the child comments that "she proved to be a touchy person"). There is an almost continuous "flattening" of language, a sort of ironic, poignantly amusing "neutrality" in the child's reportorial mode (he reports the sudden death of his father, for example, in the same tone and with the same brevity that he uses to describe shop windows), his unusual use of verbal aspect (especially his employment of perfectives formed with the prefix *po-* to reduce simple reportage such as "maman cried" or "maman was crying" to "maman had a little cry"), and his misplacement of expected word order. Sentences, for instance, frequently end with a verb, but lack its expected qualification or amplification ("a raft, its oar squeaking, floated"). Sometimes a key adjective is mislocated to a position where it carries either more or less than its anticipated weight ("Nannies with country hairdos, wearing dark jackets, *fat*, were sitting"; my emphasis).

All of this combines to create a richly nuanced exposition of the child's epistemological and emotional relationship to the experiences he is narrating, and of the author's ironic regard for his child's narrative. Also included in these stylistic expressions of psychology are Dobychin's failure to mark reported speech in quotation marks and his odd use of accent marks (the latter a feature of style that is not translatable). The seemingly promiscuous use of quotation marks, for example, is particularly effective in conveying the child's insecurity regarding his understanding of what certain words signify and what his attitude toward them should be, be they a room in his friend's apartment (the "boudoir"), an explanation for the absence of the mother's midwife friend (at "her practice"), or the proper facial expression to assume when adults are contemplating one and considering the question of one's developing sexuality (an "air of impenetrability"). The translators have preserved the original punctuation whenever practicable, and have endeavored to recreate in English as many equivalences as possible for the peculiarities of Dobychin's diction, syntax, and style, even when they appear to be awkward (the repetition of odd adjectives, strangely placed: "she came running, squattish"; the separation of subject and predicate by long qualifiers: "Karmanova, wearing a 'red mat-iné made from shawls with a Turkish design,' would begin scurry-ing"; the interruption of a name or quotation with awkwardly inserted narrative explanations: " 'A Dangerous—was entitled the article about fifteen-year-olds that had been printed there—Age' "); or even incorrect (the child's tendency to say "I and Serge" rather than "Serge and I").

There is, of course, much in *The Town of N* for readers to enjoy even without the knowledge necessary for penetrating some of its subtextual, intertextual, and parodic subtleties, and even for read-ers who are unwilling to do the rereading imperative for assimilat-ing some of the novel's narrative structures, its patterns, echoes, comic inversions, ironic parallels and juxtapositions. But those who, after completing a first reading of *The Town of N,* arm them-selves for further exploration by familiarizing themselves with, for instance, Gogol's *Dead Souls* or Sologub's *A Petty Demon,* the nov-els of Dostoevsky or the paintings of A. A. Ivanov, Leonardo and Raphael, or even just the outlines of early twentieth-century Russian history, will find return visits to *The Town of N* munifi-cently rewarded, and may truly appreciate the charms of Leonid Dobychin's unique genius.

Richard Chandler Borden
Paris, 1997

Notes

1. Information about Dobychin's life and works may be found in V. S. Bakhtin, "Dobychin: Shtrikhi zhizni i tvorchestva," in *Vtoraia proza: Russkaia proza 20-x - 30-x godov XX veka,* ed. W. Weststeijn, D. Rizzi, and T. V. Tsiv'ian (Trent: Dipartimento di Scienze Filologiche e Storiche, 1995). Memoir accounts of Dobychin's character and fate include Marina Chukovskaia's "Odinochestvo" and Veniamin Kaverin's "Dobychin," both in *Pisatel' Leonid Dobychin: Vospominaniia, Stat'i, Pis'ma,* ed. Vladimir Bakhtin (Saint Petersburg: AOZT "Zhurnal 'Zvezda,'" 1996), and *Vtoraia Proza.*

2. Veniamin Kaverin, *Epilog: Memuary* (Moscow, 1989), 204–5.

3. Victor Erofeyev, Introduction to *The Penguin Book of New Russian Writing: Russia's Fleurs du Mal,* ed. Victor Erofeyev and Andrew Reynolds (London and New York: Penguin, 1995).

4. One scholar, Dubravka Ugrešić ("O 'Gorode En' Leonida Dobychina," in *Pisatel' Leonid Dobychin,* 280–87), places *The Town of N* within the "childhood" context of Russian modernists such as Andrei Bely (*Kotik Letaev*), Osip Mandel'shtam ("The Noise of Time"), and Yury Olesha (stories such as "Human Material" and "I Look into the Past").

5. See, in particular, A. F. Belousov, "Zhiznennaia osnova i literaturnyi kontekst romana L. Dobychina 'Gorod En,'" in *Vtoraia proza,* 45–50, and Aleksandra Petrova, "Iz zametok o 'Gorode En': Tsitirovanie i istoriko-kul'turnyi podtekst," in *Pisatel' Leonid Dobychin,* 213–16.

6. Petrova identifies this play as N. N. Lerner's *The Death of Pushkin.*

7. A good introductory study of Dobychin's poetics is Iurii Shcheglov, "Zametki o proze Leonida Dobychina ('Gorod En')," *Literaturnoe obozrenie* 3, nos. 7/8, 25–36. He discusses many of the

stylistic idiosyncrasies, and several of the examples, cited in this paragraph. Many useful studies of Dobychin's life and art have been collected in the two volumes cited above: *Pisatel' Leonid Dobychin* and *Vtoraia proza*.

»»» «««

The Town *of* N

To Alexander Pavlovich Drozdov[*]

1

It was drizzling. The hems of maman's and Alexandra Lvovna Ley's skirts were raised slightly and fastened in several places to elastic bands with clasps, sewn onto a rubber belt. These elastic bands were called "pages." The wet cobblestones on the carriageway and the bricks on the sidewalks sparkled. Drops fell from umbrellas. On the shop signs naked brown Indians with feathers on their heads were smoking. —Don't look back—maman was telling me.

The prison castle, four stories tall, with towers, was visible up ahead. That was where they were having the feast of Our Lady of Sorrows, and we were going there to mass. Alexandra Lvovna Ley was moralizing, and maman, moved, was agreeing with her.

—No, indeed—they were saying—it would be hard to find a place where this feast would be more to the point than in a prison.

Blowing her nose, an imposing lady in a fur collar passed us, and, bringing her pince-nez to her eyes, cast over us a favorable glance. Her dark-complexioned face resembled the little illustration of "Chichikov."* At the gates everyone stopped to unfasten the "pages," and the "lady-Chichikov" looked at us once again. Rings of brown stone with sparkles hung in her ears. —Attractive—said maman of her.

We entered the church and crowded around the candle box. —For *proskomidia** —the ladies muttered, counting out change.

Father Fyodor in a gold costume with little blue posies, bowing, swung his censer toward us. I was flattered that he had greeted us so nicely. Behind the castle ran the railroad, and its whistles could be heard. In the iconostasis I noticed Our Lady. She wasn't gaunt and black, but sleek, and her kerchief puffed up prettily behind her. I liked her. From the choir the prisoners were watching us. —Stand properly—maman ordered me.

The sound of tramping rang out, and schoolgirls appeared, crossing themselves. A teacher set them in line. She crossed herself and, straightening her skirt in back, turned around to look at it. Then she screwed up her eyes, glanced in our direction, and bowed. —Madmazelle* Gorshkova—explained Alexandra Lvovna, nodding to her. The lady-Chichikov from time to time threw us glances.

Suddenly the warder brought out the lectern and coughed. Everyone stood closer. Father Fyodor came out, cleaning his nose with a handkerchief. He assumed a dignified air and delivered a sermon on the theme of sorrows.

—Don't shun them—he said. —God visits us in them. One saint had no sorrows and wept bitterly: "God has forgotten me," he grieved.

—Ah, how true it is—the ladies marveled, going out of the gates and again setting to the "pages." The rain dribbled a little. Madmazelle Gorshkova came alongside us. Alexandra Lvovna Ley presented her to us. The schoolgirls surrounded us, and, chased away by Madmazelle Gorshkova, ran off and then came skipping up again. I was indignant at them.

So we stood for several minutes. Locomotives whistled. Father Fyodor clambered up into a droshky and, giving the driver a shove in the back, rolled off. We conversed. Alexandra Lvovna Ley gesticulated and grumbled in her bass. —True, true—maman was agreeing and fluttering her hat from time to time. Madmazelle

Gorshkova wrapped herself in a feather boa, raised her eyebrows, and screwed up her eyes. Her glance stopped on me, and some sort of consideration flashed across her face. I became uneasy. The lady-Chichikov, meanwhile, reached the turn, glanced back, and disappeared around the corner.

Taking leave of Madmazelle Gorshkova, we talked about her. —Well-bred—we praised her and, coming out onto the main road, fell silent. Wheels rumbled. Shopkeepers, standing on their thresholds, called to us to come inside. —We'll stop in here—maman said suddenly, and we entered L. Kusman's bookstore. It was dark there, and smelled pleasantly of book bindings and globes. The languid L. Kusman examined us sadly with faded eyes. —I seldom see you—she said tenderly. —Give me "The Sacred Story"—maman said to her. Everyone turned and glanced at me.

L. Kusman pointed to me with her eyes, inserted a little picture into "The Sacred Story," and, nimbly wrapping the purchase, handed it over. —A ruble ten—she announced the price and then said: —For you, a ruble.

The little picture turned out to be an—"angel." All covered with varnish, it was raised in places to boot. Maman glued it onto the wallpaper in the dining room. —Let it watch over you and see that you eat properly—she said. I'd always see it during meals. —Darling—I'd lovingly think.

2

Father left for the offices where recruits are received. Not yet dressed, maman looked after the housecleaning. I got a book and read how Chichikov arrived in the town of N and how everyone took a liking to him. How they harnessed horses to the *britchka* and set off to visit the landowners, and what they ate there. How

Manilov* came to love him and, standing on the porch, dreamed that the tsar would learn of their friendship and confer generalships upon them.

—What are you so keen on there?—maman asked me. She always said that instead of "What are you reading?" —Call Cecilia—she said—and go for a stroll. —Cecilia—I shouted, and she came running, squattish. Getting her apron, she clambered to her little trunk, which was called a *"skrynka."** Music played in its lock and Leo XIII appeared. He was pasted onto the lid inside.

The day was sunny, and the street beamed. The chocolate sheep that stood in the bakery window glistened. Carts rumbled. When conversing we had to shout to understand one another. We admired a lady in the window of the barber shop and looked over religious objects in the windows of Pyotr m-ch-t Mitrofanov.* A march crashed out. A company of soldiers was approaching, and an orchestra played, sparkling. Kapellmeister Schmidt majestically waved his gloved hand. Madame Strauss in a red dress ran out of the sausage shop and, smiling blissfully, nodded endlessly to him. Wrapping herself in a shawl, L. Kusman opened her door a bit.

Shrill singing was heard, and a funeral procession appeared. A man in a shirt decorated with lace carried a cross, a Polish priest* stepped forward, all puffed up. —There—Cecilia pronounced piously and looked upward—the nannies and cooks will reign, and their masters will serve them. I did not believe this.

—This seems to be a pretty little lane—said Cecilia to me. We turned, and a Polish church came into view. Red-roofed, it shone white behind the branches. By its fence, which had receded from the street in a semicircle, sat beggars. Cecilia seized the opportunity, and we stopped in there. It was already empty, but still stank of pilgrims. Two stone women were standing by the door, and one of them resembled L. Kusman and was draped like her. We prayed to them and, falling silent, wandered about. Our footsteps boomed.

—Our faith is the true one—boasted Cecilia after we had left. I did not agree with her.

Across the road I saw a dark little boy in a window and nudged Cecilia. We stopped and looked at him. Suddenly he crossed his eyes, stuck his fingers into the corners of his mouth, and, pulling them downward, stuck out his tongue. I shrieked in terror. Cecilia covered my face with her hand. —Spit—she ordered me and crossed herself: —Jezus, Marya. We ran.

"A Frightful Boy," my father entitled this incident. Maman looked at him with annoyance. She liked to have everything treated seriously.

Alexandra Lvovna Ley had not visited us for three days already, and at dinner we spoke of her. We decided that she was "at her practice." I was given two extra helpings of *kissel,** the more quickly to restore my strength, shaken by fright. On the wall before me was the angel from L. Kusman. It stood on a cloud, holding a palm branch. A star shone over its head.

Prziborowski, the medical assistant, reported. With his hair standing on end and a broad mustache, he resembled the picture "Nietzsche." Rising, father ordered him to clean the instruments and left the room. —Into Morphia's embrace—Prziborowski explained respectfully, bowing after him. —Make yourself comfortable here—commanded maman, remaining at the table. —It's not worth lighting a second lamp. —Verily—answered Prziborowski.

Various tongs and scissors sparkled. —Today—he said while cleaning—I happened to be in the Polish church. The sermon was wonderful. And he recounted it: how we should obey, and discharge our duties. —It's true—maman agreed magnanimously and became thoughtful. —After all, there's but one God—she said— only faiths are different. —Exactly so—Prziborowski was deeply moved. He beamed.

Thus did Alexandra Lvovna Ley find us discoursing. We were glad, warmed up dinner for her, and questioned her about who'd been born. At seven o'clock I was put to bed and shut my eyes. Suddenly that frightful boy appeared to me. I leaped up. The ladies came running in, got all excited, and, until I fell asleep, sat near to me and quietly conversed. —No, but Leykin*—I heard, half-asleep. —Did you read about how they got lost in Paris, so they hired a cabby and told him the address? And in a whisper they laughed.

3

Snow covered the cobblestones. It grew still. We sacked Cecilia. She had put down our religion, and this had become known to maman.

The lock on the *skrynka* played its music, Pope Leo appeared once again—in a skullcàp and cape. Touched, I decided to bid Cecilia a friendly farewell and make her an offering of bread and salt.* I salted a piece of bread and held it out to her, but she pushed it away.

Kagan the factoress sent us a new nanny. She was of the Uniates,* and everyone liked this. —There's even a medal—guests would tell us—in honor of the abolishment of the union. Christmas came. Maman smiled and went about pleased. —It reminds me of childhood—she repeated over and over.

She was invited to the Belugins to meet the New Year. Wonderfully coiffed and curled, she stood straight beside the mirror. Two candles illumined her. Standing up on a chair, I fastened the dress hooks on her back. Father was already in his frock coat. He sprinkled us with perfume from an atomizer. —How lighthearted—said maman, coming up to him and taking him by

»»»» 8 ««««

the arm. —Why is that? We haven't won two hundred thousand, have we?

While being undressed by the nanny, I thought about what we should do with these winnings. We could buy ourselves a *britchka* and roll off to the town of N. They'd love us there. I'd become friends there with Themistoclius and Alcides Manilov.*

Morning was pleasant. The night watchmen from the office, chimney sweeps, and bathhouse attendants came by and congratulated us on the New Year. —All right, all right—we said to them and gave them ruble notes. The mailman brought a heap of postcards and envelopes with visiting cards: orchestras of angels played violins, men in tailcoats and ladies with trains clinked glasses, stamped over our acquaintances' names and patronymics were crowns.

Maman, smiling, sat down beside me. —Last night—she said—I made the acquaintance of a lady who has a little boy by the name of Serge. You will become friends. Tomorrow he is going to visit us. She rose, looked at the thermometer, and sent me and the nanny out to stroll.

It smelled of snow. Crows screamed. Cabbies' nags ran past in no hurry. It dripped from the rooftops. —What if Serge is one of them—the nanny and I were saying regarding those boys whom we liked. Fat Strauss sped past wearing a gray jacket and a little cap with a green plumelet. He drove with one hand, and with the other held Madame Strauss at the small of the back. The bells in the cathedral were ringing, and everyone was heading in that direction—to watch the parade.

After jostling in the crowd, we found ourselves a place. Soldiers stamped their feet. Policemen on big horses, riding into the crowd, moved it back. The bells began to ring out. Everyone started. Stooped over, banners appeared in the doorways and straightened up. The prayer service had ended. The parade began. Someone gave me a fillip on the back of the head. It was a pupil, wearing a coat with gilt buttons. He was no longer looking at me. Head lifted, he was following the movement of the clouds. He reminded me of our angel (on the wallpaper in the dining room), and I was moved. —Dearest—I thought.

We returned in military step to the sounds of the retiring music. Father, having made the rounds with New Year's greetings, met up with us. He sat me in the sleigh and gave me a lift. The nanny ran after us.

When we arrived, a visitor was sitting on the sofa in the living room. Maman was receiving him, holding herself erect. He twirled the ashtray "Dreyfus reads a journal" and told us about how in Petersburg rubber tires had appeared. —You'll be walking along— he said—and see cabbies' droshkies rushing about noiselessly.

At dinner we regretted that Alexandra Lvovna wasn't with us. We sent Prziborowski for her, but she, poor dear, turned out to be at her practice.

Guests arrived in the evening, and we told them about the rubber tires. —Scientific progress—they marveled. Bearded, like in "The Sacred Story," they sat down to cards. Father seemed so young among them. —Pass—they declared. One of them was a "bye," and maman entertained him. —Yesterday I made the acquaintance—she said—of Karmanova, the engineer's missus. She is a very pleasant woman. Not for nothing was it, then, that as I was getting ready to go to the Belugins I was full of bright presentiments. She'll be visiting us tomorrow. —And Serge too—said I.

The hour of their arrival had come at last. The little bell rang. I ran out. A lamp burned in the foyer. Maman already was exclaiming delight. Before her, sniffling and freeing themselves from their fur coats, smiled the lady-Chichikov and the "Frightful Boy."

4

They liked the angel in the dining room. The engineer's missus examined it businesslike through her pince-nez and said it came from abroad. I was glad. She glanced about complacently. She wore a jacket of blue velvet with spangles, the brooch "assembly of love," and a sash with a "lyre" clasp. —Are you going to the fortress?— she asked: —On Saturdays an *akathistus** is held there.

Serge was wearing a green suit. He took me by the hand, and, leading me away, showed me that the fastening of his trousers was located in front.

—Like grown-ups—I marveled. He and I chatted a bit. —Serge—I asked him after looking around—was it you who once made a frightful face at me? He swore that it wasn't. I was touched.

Father came out to tea when the guests had departed. Terribly pleased, maman hummed and with a sly look chuckled. —You know— she said—she and I have agreed to reread all of Leykin together.

I, too, was happy. Leaving them, I secretly made off for the living room. There I settled quietly next to the stove and heard the pine needles falling. Through the window, the lantern illuminated the branch of a fir tree. On it sparkled silver rain. —Serge, Serge, oh, Serge—I repeated.

Later on maman and I visited them. We kissed in the foyer. The engineer's missus presented to us her daughter, the secondary-school girl Sophie Samokvasova. —Very pleased—said Sophie. Taking each other by the waist, the ladies went through to the engineer's missus's room, called the "boudoir." I shook Serge's hand: —You and I—we're like Manilov and Chichikov. He had not read about them. I told him how they had become friends and how they had wanted to live together and the two of them study sciences.

Serge opened a bookcase and got out his books. We began looking through them. —Here's Don Quixote—Serge showed me: —he was a fool. Just before tea Sophie Samokvasova did a scarf dance for us. —Wonderful—said maman, applauding. —Is Serge nice?—she asked as we were returning. —Yes, he's a well-bred boy—I answered her.

Alexandra Lvovna we now regarded without interest when she stopped by. She promised to get us an album of samples of the Saratov factory's printed calico. We told her about our friendship with the Karmanovs.

A few days later we saw each other at the blessing of the waters.* The sun already gave off a little warmth. Standing on the dike, we screwed up our eyes. Gonfalons stirred below. The priests' toilette dazzled. The firs darkened. When they started firing the cannons, Sophie Samokvasova ran up from somewhere, dragging with her the engineer Karmanov. He was shorter than the ladies. —Very glad—he exclaimed, making his bows. He wore a uniform cap. There were anchors and axes on his buttons. His beard was disheveled and appeared unkempt. —The blessing of the water went off very nicely—he said and winked at me from behind his pince-nez. Taking his leave, he invited me to the railroad's Christmas party.

After parting with him, the five of us strolled along the dike in the direction of the fortress. Visible was its white cathedral with the two towers. Very narrow, from a distance they resembled candles. —They say it's a former Polish church—Sophie Samokvasova told us. The ladies, carried away with their conversation on religious themes, fell behind. I conversed with Serge, giggling. Some grand lady sped past us, with a soldier on the coachbox. We glanced at each other and chuckled, and Serge taught me a ditty:

Poor Madame Fou-Fou's
Head's got a screw loose.
Dressed as always à la mode.
But has her head in the commode.

Father was in the regional capital that day. Maman was silent at dinner. Pleasantly lost in reverie, she sometimes smiled. —The days are getting noticeably longer—she said.

A man drove up from the Karmanovs. We questioned him. It turned out that his name was Ludwig Chaplinsky and that he served at the depot. He took me away. Serge and the engineer were awaiting me.

In that same cab we set off for the theater. The military orchestra was playing there under the direction of Kapellmeister Schmidt. Multicolored lights shone on the Christmas tree. The engineer informed us that they were—electric. We were each brought a toy horse, and we dispatched Chaplinsky to bring them home.

Serge had been here before. He knew everything. He brought me up to the stage and explained that the picture on the curtain was named "Chillon Castle." —Listen—he said to me suddenly—it was I who made that frightful face at you then.

Afterward he swore that it had not been he.

5

The Karmanovs moved to Janek's house and occupied an apartment of ten rooms. The biggest was called the "hall." It was proposed that at Shrovetide a performance be given in it with a real curtain from the theater. On Sundays boy and girl pupils would come and rehearse. I and Serge once spied a teensy bit. Sophie was on her knees before Kolya Lieberman, reaching out her hands to him. —Alexander—she said touchingly—oh, forgive me.

The Belugins were transferred to Mitau. Upon leaving, they turned their apartment in Janek's house over to us. Now we could see the Karmanovs every day. They sent us Chaplinsky—to help with the move. To maman's chagrin, Father wouldn't receive him. Prziborowski, packing up our things, sympathized with her.

The angel L. Kusman had treated me to wouldn't come unstuck, and we had to leave it behind. I was very sorry. I kissed it. Guests began visiting us to bring us housewarming greetings and give us pretzels and pies. A gentleman who had died in the house appeared at night to maman. —You can just imagine—she said. On the advice of Alexandra Lvovna Ley we called in Father Fyodor. He held a prayer service. Alexandra Lvovna Ley and the engineer's missus and Serge attended. A little yellow table was covered with a napkin. An icon and water in a salad bowl were placed on it. After chanting a while, as in church, Father Fyodor went around to all the rooms and blessed them. We accompanied him. Coffee was served.

Kagan the factoress once again searched for a nanny for us. The Uniate had been rude and maman had sent her packing. That evening, anxious, she didn't read Leykin with the engineer's missus, but conversed with her about servants. Alexandra Lvovna Ley stopped by. —A find—she shouted, unwrapping something. We saw a little picture: Jesus Christ wearing a crown of thorns. —Wonderful—we approved. —The fact is—said Alexandra Lvovna—that while leaving home she had met the dressmaker Pani Plepis. Every time she sees her something good happens. Now we had a talk about lucky encounters.

Shrovetide neared. They were already baking trial pancakes.

Serge and I composed a play and went to ask Sophie to be a spectator. Her friend Elsa Budrikh was visiting her. They made eyes at one another and performed a pas.

—Come along, come along, angel dearest—they sang in their little voices—

Come dance the polka sublime.
Hear, do you hear the sounds of the polka,
The sounds of the polka divine.

We invited them. On the stage was a *britchka*. The horses were running. Selifan* was lashing them. We were silent. Manilovka awaited us, and at Manilovka—Alcides and Themistoclius, standing on the porch, holding hands.

Suddenly the engineer's missus appeared in the spectators' room. —Sophie—she said, approaching the girls—Ivan Fomich is here. He has made an offer. I was sorry that our performance had been ruined. Outside snow was falling. You could see the chimney atop Sechenkova's commercial bathhouse. Smoke was coming from it.

Ivan Fomich served as inspector of the technical school. We began visiting the school church. Up front the pupils stood modestly. In the middle the bearded teachers, wearing uniforms with university badges and crew cuts, crossed themselves. Returning home, the ladies spoke flatteringly of them and praised them for their piety. Serge now loved to play "school," and the engineer's missus began reporting the school news. Thus we learned of the sixth-form pupil Vasya Strizhkin. During physics he had lit up a little cigar and, with his parents' consent, had been flogged.

Winter ended. Chief of Police Lomov had already made his final rounds by sleigh and had given the order to remove the snow.

Again droshkies began to rumble. Our mothers fasted and brought us with them to church. On the cathedral ceiling there was a sky with little clouds and stars. I liked to examine it.

Once the engineer's missus and Serge called on us. She had heard about some very advantageous candies—"caramel Merci"— that were available at Kryukov's shop beyond the dike. We made our way there. The sun was shining. People with red physiognomies were coming out of the commercial baths. Women selling kvass were stopping them. The apothecary shop was here too. Soap and bast washmops displayed themselves vividly in the shop window. We came upon the pupil who had given me the fillip on the back of the head at the New Year's parade. He was walking along, whistling.

We liked the caramels "Merci." On their wrappers there were two hands that greeted one another. They were on the smallish side, and there were lots of them to a pound. While Serge and the ladies watched the weighing out, the Kryukov daughter called me aside and gave me a gingerbread woman.

6

The earth had already dried out. The yardman had already raked and burned last year's leaves. L. Kusman had already put Easter postcards on display in her window.

Once after dinner I was taking a walk around the yard. Serge came out. —Tomorrow we're going to the fortress—he announced—and you're coming with us. It turned out that the engineer's missus planned to go there to pray for the late Samokvasov.

Bom, the bells in the cathedral began ringing. We crossed ourselves. Pferdchen came up to the window with a whistle and whistled. His children went running home. —*Kinder*—we cried after th_m—*tey trrinken**—and then we fell into a reverie, listening to the ringing. We had a talk about those stupidities that they say about grown-ups. We doubted that gentlemen and ladies would do such things. An organ-grinder called in, and cheerful music began turning somersaults in the air. It roused us. —Let's go see the basement people—Serge proposed to me.

We groped our way down, and, guiding ourselves by hand along the wall, found the doors. At the basement people's it stank of paupers. Geraniums bloomed in tin boxes in their windows. In a corner with pictures, as in Cecilia's *skrynka,* was Pope Leo, smiling, with little narrow shoulders. The basement people awoke and looked up at us from the bench. —Your children won't leave us alone—we complained, as always. —We'll show them—the basement people told us, as always.

Serge, the engineer's missus, and Sophie came by for us in the morning. We sent Prziborowski for the droshky. He seated us and, admiring us, followed us with a bow.

The day was drab. Bells were ringing. German women, all dressed up, hurried to the Protestant church arm in arm with their husbands, and the gilded edges of their Psalters gleamed from under their arms. Thundering, we galloped off across the cobblestones. Then the cab climbed onto the dike and began to rumble more quietly. From up high we could see mattresses that had been dragged out into the yards having the dust beaten from them. The river flowed broadly. —Nature is awakening—Sophie was saying poetically, and the ladies agreed.

The fortress came into view. Jackdaws were screaming above its trees. Horses roamed along the earthen walls. Water glistened in the moats. Above the water little windows with gratings could be seen. We took a good look at them—perhaps someone would peep out from there. On the drawbridges the wheels would stop rumbling. Suddenly it would become quiet, and the hooves would click. We would be reminded of the stories about rubber tires.

Descending from the cab, we stood a while in the middle of the square and marveled at the beauty of the cathedral. Before us was a little square enclosed by chains. These chains were fastened to decorative cannons, set with muzzles pointing upward, and dangled between them.

I caught sight of the New Year's pupil (the one who gave me the fillip) on a little bench. He was sitting, stroking a willow branch with catkins. Sophie giggled. —There's Vasya Strizhkin—she pointed. —Vasya—I said in a whisper. He glanced at us. I stood gaping and, falling behind the ladies, stumbled and found a five-kopeck piece.

The next day Yankel the panoramaist appeared in our yard, playing his guitar. Now I gave up my five-kopeck piece and, together with the panorama, I was covered with something black, as if I were a photographer. —*Ei, zwei, drei**—said Yankel from outside. I saw everything that I'd heard so much about—both "The Expulsion from Paradise" and "The Family of Alexander III." People stood around and envied me.

On the Saturday before Easter, when the Easter cakes were already baking in the oven, maman shut herself up with me in the bedroom and, sitting down on the bed, read me the Gospels. "The Beloved Pupil"* interested me in particular. I imagined him wearing a little coat with gold buttons, whistling, and holding a branch of pussy willow.

The evening mailman had already brought us several post- and visiting cards. —*Pan Khristus z martvekh vsta**—Prziborowski wrote us—*alelyuya, alelyuya, alelyuya.*

I awoke in the middle of the night, when everybody was coming back from matins. I was allowed to get up. Solemn, we ate. Alexandra Lvovna Ley took part.

The morning was sunny, with little clouds, like on that postcard with the bunny that Madmazelle Gorshkova had unexpectedly sent us. The pealing of bells came flying in the windows. Guests rolled up rumbling in cabs, and, prickling us with their beards, greeted us. Maman beamed. —Come and have something to eat—she told them. Hands behind his back, Father wandered about. —*Pan Khristus z martvekh vsta*—he hummed, content. Father Fyodor rolled up and, after dragging out a prayer, blessed the food.

After dinner the Kondratyevs and their children came to visit. Andrey was my age. He had a white bow with little green dots and his hair stood on end like Nietzsche's and Prziborowski's. I wanted to make friends with him, but faithfulness to Serge held me back.

7

I saw Janek. The chestnut trees were in bloom. The sun was low. The fleecy clouds were colored pink and violet. In a top hat, squattish, with a little triangular gray beard, he gave orders as he went. Kantorek the manager accompanied him. I told maman of this encounter, and she fell into a reverie. —I've never seen him—she said, but Father shrugged his shoulders. He didn't like people who were richer than we were. He wouldn't get acquainted with the Karmanovs either, even though maman was constantly badgering him.

The Kondratyevs dropped by to bid us farewell and moved to the encampments. They invited us, and one morning, all decked out, we sent for a cab, took our seats, and set out for there. We passed the baths, the Kryukov shop, and Tekla Andruszkiewicz's haberdashery concern. Hanging in its little window were candles bound at the wick and a cotton Christmas tree old lady with cranberries. The paving came to an end. It became pleasant. Gardeners worked in the muck beyond the wattle fences. Larks sang. The forest could be seen up ahead, and martial music drifted over from there. —It's the encampments—maman told us.

The Kondratyevs' barrack stood near the entrance. A gold mirrored sphere glittered on a post. Rakhmatulla the orderly was doing a wash.

Kondratyeva, jumping up off the swing, ran over to us. We praised the garden and climbed up onto the veranda. There I spotted a book with inscriptions in the margins. "To each his own!" had been written in indelible pencil and wetted. "Oho!" —"Thus Spake"—maman read out the title—"Zarathustra." —It's my husband who reads and makes notes—Kondratyeva told us. Andrey came and showed me a kite onto which Edward VII in a Scottish kilt had been glued.

We set off to roam a bit and surveyed the encampments. We came upon Andrey's father. Long, with a little face and narrow trunk, he was sitting in a droshky and was draped in an overcoat flung over one shoulder. —Off to see a patient in town—he shouted to us. We stopped to wave to him. —When they flog a soldier, he attends—said Andrey. The orchestra, drawing nearer, was playing marches. Cadets sped by on bicycles, not holding onto the handlebars. Mobile kitchens rattled and gave off the smell of cabbage soup.

Suddenly a little storm cloud gathered, rain sprinkled and began to beat against the burdocks. We waited it out beneath a sentry mushroom. I read a poster on the mushroom's column: variety show, orchestra, the vaudeville *His Orderly Put Him on the Spot*. I told Andrey how I'd once been in a theater, how electricity, multicolored, shone on the Christmas tree, and how a chillon castle was depicted on the curtain. I told about my friendship with Serge, about Manilov and Chichikov, and about how even now I didn't know who the "Frightful Boy" was—Serge or not Serge.

—And you'll never find out—said Andrey. —Yes—I agreed

with him—yes! Thus conversing, we descended to the shore. The river was brown. A raft, its oar squeaking, floated. Beyond the river stretched low, plowed-up hills. Kolya Lieberman was bathing. He was standing, stern, holding himself up to the sun, and I recalled how Sophie had gazed at him, genuflecting. —Oh, Alexander—she had exclaimed, repenting and wringing her hands—oh, forgive me. She hadn't seen how fat-fleshed he is and how shaggy from head to toe. —Yes, yes—Andrey replied to this—yes! Profound, we remained silent. Marches resounded from behind. Fish sometimes plashed. With a battledore and a pile of linen, like a laundress, Rakhmatulla came out onto the plank footway.

Ahead lay separation from Serge. He was leaving for the summer for Samokvasovo with the engineer's missus and Sophie.

The day of their departure arrived. Maman and I showed up at the station with candies. Ivan Fomich, Chaplinsky, the engineer, and Elsa Budrikh were seeing them off. We saw the dressmaker Pani Plepis, surrounded by bundles, apart from the travelers. She was going with the Karmanovs to make the trousseau. She was standing in a red hat, squattish, and glancing about. The engineer had arranged for them to open the "imperial rooms" for us. —It's very nice here—he praised, sitting down on a gilded chair. We were brought champagne, and the engineer's missus darkened. —That's excessive—she said. Nevertheless, we drank up and shouted "hurrah!" Sophie was pleased. —Like in a novel—she compared, licking her lips and becoming a little drowsy. She had graduated from the gymnasium and already dressed as a lady. Wearing a floor-length skirt, a corset, a hat with feathers, and balloon sleeves, she had become clumsy and imposing.

We returned home limp. —All the same—maman was saying to me, settling against the back of the cab and smiling tenderly—she is a bit stingy. I dozed. I thought about the dressmaker Pani Plepis, and about the luck encounters with her bring Alexandra Lvovna. I recalled my own encounters with Vasya, the five-kopeck piece I found in the fortress, and the gingerbread the Kryukov daughter gave me.

8

Summer we spent in the country on the Courland coast. From our windows we could see the river with a ferry and a little town on the other side. A Polish church stood on the hill. To the side a flagstaff without a flag stuck out from behind the verdure. This was the "palazzo."

Alexandra Lvovna Ley, leaving a substitute's address on her door, sometimes visited us. Festive, wearing a suit of Saratov print-ed calico, an "Amazon" hat, and a "chain" charm bracelet, she would breathe noisily: —To better ventilate the lungs—she'd explain to us. Maman told her about how the count had caught two peasant women mushroom picking in his forest and had beaten them up, and she was indignant.

I saw him once. I had set off for the little town with the nanny to buy *baranki*.* Bathers were swimming up to the ferry and grabbing ahold of the rope. A carriage in four, its varnish gleaming, descend-ed to the shore. The coachman was wearing a two-layered cape with silver buttons. The count was smoking. —They're Catholics—said the nanny and, excited, hurried to call at the Polish church. I, too, was touched.

Haymaking had already come and gone. Madame Strauss visited the pharmacist von Bonin's missus, and while she was staying there Kapellmeister Schmidt came by rather often. Time flew. Already we were sitting down to supper by lamplight. Finally Prziborowski reported and we began to pack.

A cabby rolled up and said "bonjour." He informed us that some military fares had taught him that. We started off. Our landlords stood and followed us with their eyes. It was pleasant and sad. The little bell tinkled. —Good-bye, cross at the turning—we said— farewell, stork.

In the evening, the engineer's missus was already sitting in our apartment and maman was telling her how before going to sleep she'd run across the kitchen garden down to the river wearing only a cloak. She would bathe, and the cook, holding a sheet, would stand by the water, ready to be of service and barely visible in the dark.

Again guests began visiting us. The ladies were interested in the count and asked questions about his looks. The gentlemen played vint. Gray-bearded, they'd converse about the talking machine invented in the United States and about the fact that electric lighting must be injurious to the eyes.

Maman conferred with some of them. She decided that I had to begin writing. She loved to consult. We looked in on L. Kusman and bought some copybooks there. As always, L. Kusman muffled herself up and huddled, doleful and languid. —Summer passes— she said to us—and you stand and watch it from behind the counter. —That's true—maman answered her. I felt sad, and, coming home, asked to go into the garden in order to think, off by myself, about the writing that lay before me. The leaves already were turning yellow. The sky was faded. Nannies with country hairdos, wearing dark jackets, fat, were sitting beneath the chestnut trees and singing all together in thin little voices:

An unfortunate creature
The Orlov conductor.
The ink's his estate,
But the brake is his home.

Having seen me from a window, Serge came running out. He told me that the bishop was coming from Vitebsk and after the service would be distributing crosses with little diamonds. —If we get them—I said—then we can exchange them, Serge, as a mark of our friendship.

Soon he arrived and officiated in the cathedral. We attended. While dressing, before putting anything on, he would put it to his lips. The crosses he gave out were tin plate, and we gave them away to the beggars.

It was somebody's name day at the Kondratyevs. There was a crush and confusion. I slipped away to the "drawing room." It smelled of iodoform there. "A Panorama of Reval" and the "Zarathustra" with inscriptions in the margins lay on a table. Andrey found me there. We had a talk. It was nice being with him and, since I already had a friend, I doubted whether this were permissible.

Whenever she visited us now Alexander Lvovna would question us about Sophie's marriage, which had recently taken place. —September—she would begin to count on her fingers, preoccupied, jingling the charms on her bracelet. Then she would smile and become pensive. —Interesting, interesting—she'd say to us.

Once I was writing after dinner. The sun lit up the garden. The window was open. Pferdchen voices could be heard. "The caftans," I copied from the writing sample, "are green." —Drop that—said Father. He was getting ready to visit a patient and asked me to join him. It was a warm evening. Already the electricity on the bridge was alight. A freight train, letting out puffs, shunted below, where the factory shops Karmanov commanded clustered, dark with soot. On the hill stood a Protestant church with a rooster on its steeple. Here the dike ended and turned into a street.

It was already dark when we were returning. The stars already were out, and the cabbies already were lighting the coachbox lanterns. Suddenly we heard some unfamiliar sort of noise. Stopping, we turned. A droshky rolled past us without a sound. Its wheels didn't rattle, and there was only the clicking of hooves. We looked at one another and listened some more. —Rubber tires—we spoke at last.

9

That fall Father was infected doing a postmortem and died. Until his bearing-away to the church our front door was unlocked, and everyone could come in. The basement people all called numerous times. Instead of chasing them away, the cook and the nanny would run out and, surrounding themselves with them, would stand there and report all sorts of information about us.

There was a crush at the funeral service, and an amiable lady from Vitebsk, who had come specially for the burial, picked up her train, led me off to the side, and found room for us by the crucifix. The John by the cross, nice-looking, reminded me of Vasya. Deeply moved, I became lost in contemplation of the wounds of Jesus Christ and thought about how Vasya, too, had suffered. Father Fyodor on this occasion gave an interesting sermon: he addressed maman, called her by name and patronymic, just as when visiting, and said to her "thou." —God has sent thee sorrow—he said—and in it has visited thee. There was a saint who had no sorrows, and over this he wept.

In the evening, when the last guests had departed and only the lady from Vitebsk remained, and had begun to remove the dress with the train and her hair, we saw that our apartment was now too big for us.

Maman found another, not far from the Protestant church, and we moved there. Our new house was wooden, with a mezzanine and external shutters. Over the door across the road there hung a copper pretzel, and displayed in the window there was a white Polish church with pillars and statues, from out of which came a pair of newlyweds, very well-dressed. I volunteered to run out for rolls, and the shop assistant told me that it was all made out of—sugar.

While unpacking we regretted that we no longer had Prziborowski, and maman, turning around, had a little cry. When it was already dark, the whistles in the factory shops began to hoot, and we heard the factory hands begin to run down the street past our windows. Maman got up and slammed the window shut, because their reek of machine oil and soot was coming into the house.

We soon sacked the nanny and the cook, and in place of them came Rosalia, recommended by the factoress Kagan. She often sang and, whenever she did, she'd always open the prayer book, even though she didn't know how to read.

When setting off for the cemetery, we'd send her for a cab, and she'd ride home on it from the cab stand. We usually went to the cemetery toward evening, and it was quiet there, and we'd say that it felt like winter's coming.

At "I. Stupel's Monument Workshop" maman ordered a railing and a gravestone. On the wall there I noticed a picture that looked like the rosy-cheeked Mother of God from the prison church. "Madonna," was printed beneath it, "of Saint Sixtus."*

Karmanov set maman up as an apprentice at the telegraph. Putting on her black hat with the tail, she would leave, I would write, and Rosalia would serve me tea, like an adult.

After the holidays I was faced with beginning to prepare for the first form. Maman had visited Gorshkova's with me and had reached an agreement. Gorshkova lived at the school. She opened the door to us, wearing a red housecoat. The walls of the front hall were lined with coat stands. Printed on the wallpaper were pagodas with multistoried roofs. —We've come to you on business—said maman, and she received us in the sitting room. I sat up straight on the sofa. Sunset could be seen through the windows, and I was thinking that, probably, that's the very color of Navarino flame and smoke.*

Christmas came and went. At the Kondatyevs I received a cardboard thing portraying the Admiralty.* I liked it. When left alone, I would look at it and picture to myself the wonderful buildings in the town of N.

The lady from Vitebsk informed us in a long letter of what she had been doing since she had stayed with us. "I still recall," she wrote by the way, "the little wreath that Karmanova, the engineer's missus, laid on the grave." —Ah—said maman, smiling.

Snow fell on New Year's. Callers drove about. I wandered a while near the Protestant church, and through the walls could hear the organ playing within.

The mailman stopped bringing us "The Russian Gazette" and began bringing "The Stock Exchange News." Maman looked through the drawing, but so far we still hadn't won a thing. She had to keep going to the telegraph. After a few days she showed me how to tie together notebooks and textbooks, and led me away. —Nevertheless—she was saying along the way—the days have become noticeably longer. We parted by the porch. I pulled the bell. The watchwoman admitted me. I saw the Sinitsyn kid, wearing beads, and the watchwoman's son at Gorshkova's. Gorshkova was teaching them. —"In vain"—she was telling them—means "for nothing." She had me sit down, and we began to write.

10

Hanging over the bed were a carpet with a picture of a Spanish woman and Spanish men playing guitars, and a pale slipper for a clock, covered with little shells. Madmazelle Gorshkova would sometimes lie down, languid, and light a cigarette. —"Seal skins"—she would dictate and blow smoke rings—"are used for knapsacks." The watchwoman's Osip's slate pencil would squeak. He wrote on a slate board so as not to waste exercise books. Sinitsyna would make blots on her paper and, stooping, would lick them off. The watchwoman would come in, light the lamp, and its cardboard shade would throw a shadow across our faces. Then, Madmazelle Gorshkova would pull her chair up to me and under cover of the table would seize my hand and not let it go.

Sometimes, on my way to study, I'd come upon the Pferdchens. Wearing fur coats with capes, they marched in step. Once I saw Prziborowski. He noticed me from far away and turned into some gate. When I had passed, he came out.

I also came across Vasya Strizhkin once. I thought that now something good would happen. And true enough, that evening my penmanship turned out a success and the next day Madmazelle Gorshkova gave me an "A" for it.

Alexandra Lvovna Ley stopped me once on the street. —Lenten—she said in her bass, glancing at the heavens—stars— and then she asked me when it was the engineer's missus visited us.

The snow already was melting. The rooster and the hens went about the courtyard with red combs and snarled as they do in spring. On my name day I received a letter from Vitebsk. The Karmanovs came by, and Alexandra Lvovna Ley began asking how Sophie was feeling. —Why don't you go visit her—said the engineer's missus. The Kondratyevs arrived. Instead of congratulating me on my "angel's day," Andrey congratulated me on my "saint's day." —Angels are something else entirely—he explained. The ladies were not pleased. —It's not for you to be the judge of that— they began saying. Karmanova was indignant. —For tricks like that one ought to be flogged and salted—she would later say.

On the first of April we were free and set off to visit her. It was cheerful walking through the streets. —You have a worm on your head—people would try to trick one another. Whispering about Sophie and Alexandra Lvovna Ley, mysterious, the ladies retired to the "boudoir" and let me and Serge go into the garden. There, as before, nannies sat beneath the chestnut trees. From the courtyard the basement kids were spying through the fence. —What idiots— we had a talk about them. Suddenly the Pferdchen Edith came running up, out of breath. —Gentlemen—she shouted, gesticulating—they're going to beat Karl. Who wants to listen? I opened the window. We rushed after her. Coming toward us from the gate was a slender girl, who was glancing with amazement. She somehow reminded me of the Mother of God from the prison church and I. Stupel's Monument Workshop. The French governess Madame Sourir accompanied her. —Who's that?—I asked Serge on the run. —Tusenka Siou*—he answered.

It was already dark when I was walking home with maman. There were little clouds and stars in the sky, as on the cathedral ceiling. On the viaduct we ran into Kolya Lieberman. Stern, he stood looking at the lights below, and I pictured Tusenka Siou—on her knees, gazing woefully at me and exclaiming: —Alexander, oh, forgive me.

Soon I was introduced to her. One day after dinner Chaplinsky knocked at our door. He informed us that a little boy had been born to Sophie. Roused, we hastily dressed and sent for a cab.

Again maman sat with the engineer's missus in the boudoir, and me and Serge were sent out into the garden. Just as before, Tusenka appeared, escorted by Madame. Serge bowed to her. Blushing, she nodded. The shadow of a branch of bursting buds fell upon her. I looked at Serge. —This is the son of a telegraphist—he presented me.

On the day before the examinations Madmazelle Gorshkova told me how even during that first meeting with us she had suddenly sensed that I would be coming to her. A poetic expression appeared on her face. She said that she'd be bored without me. —Let's go into the garden—she bid me, having gotten rid of Sinitsyna and Osip. —Look, the apples are blossoming. —No, it's time I went, thank you—I answered. She came out to see me off. At the corner I looked back, and there she was, imposing and sad, still standing on the porch blowing smoke rings.

Maman was on duty. Rosalia served me tea. I went out and set off to take the examination, trembling. The sun was already burning. Dust rustled and flew about. Ice cream vendors wearing aprons stood on the corners. In the doorway of the sausage shop I saw Madame Strauss. Kapellmeister Schmidt was conversing with her softly. A gilded ham, gleaming, cast its blessing upon them. Vasya Strizhkin, a lilac branch behind his ear, stopped and looked at them. I prayed to him. —Vasenka—I said and crossed myself imperceptibly—help me.

11

The junior captain Chigildeev's missus lived above us in the mezzanine, and at the end of winter we made her acquaintance in order to share cabs to the cemetery. When summer came, we grew closer to her. In the morning she would come down into the garden. After standing a while over the little flower bed, she would seat herself on a collapsible walking stick–chair and would move together with it as the shade shifted. Raw-boned, wearing a brown housecoat with yellow flowers and a yellow ruche at the collar, she looked like a certain picture with the inscription "All in the Past."* —What are you reading there?—she'd sometimes ask me, and I'd show it to her.

—These are books for grown-ups—she once told me, and went

up to her place and brought me a book for children. "Favor for Favor" was how this book in a gold binding was called. Written on it was that it had been given in recognition of progress to a schoolgirl graduated to the third form. Susanna's parents belonged to the nobility, it said in it. The weather was good and they organized a picnic. The daughter of the city's mayor, Elizabeth, was also invited, although she did not belong to the nobility. She enjoyed herself there. So when the empress planned to visit this city, the mayor made efforts to see to it that Susanna was authorized to deliver the welcoming address and present the flowers.

The days passed one after the other, monotonous. Rosalia left us. —You sure do drill a lot—she had announced to us. We got angry at her for this and in reckoning deducted for the shoes given her for Easter. After her Evgenia, an Orthodox believer, came to work for us. She was a lickspittle.

The woods that began beyond Vileykskaya Street were fenced in. They were near us and we could hear the thudding of axes in them from morning to evening. Maman learned from someone that there was going to be an exhibition there. We were very interested in it, and when it opened we headed over there.

The after-dinner sun warmed us. At the edge of the sky a little cloud in the shape of a herring was motionless. Chigildeeva was fanning herself. Maman was not wearing a hat. Smartly dressed-up people passed us. A landowner rolled past on a droshky, jumped down near the exhibition, turned around, said "*prosze*"* and assisted his lady, wearing mitts and carrying a lorgnette, to descend. On the shield over the entrance a horseman was tearing along. He was wearing a helmet and chain armor. The music was playing a march.

We examined the livestock, the sacks of flour, the poultry, the exhibits of Count Plyater-Ziberg and the exhibits of Countess Broel-Plyater, called in at a pavilion with religious objects and each selected a little icon as a souvenir. Coming out, we stood a while by a pond with a little fountain and a willow tree. Its leaves had already begun to thin out a bit. —Autumn, autumn is near—we nodded our heads. Suddenly a bell rang out, and on a shed, from the doors of which they were shouting "hurry come see," a sign made up of colored lights began to shine: "Living Photography." There were separate tickets to it; we conferred and bought them.

Inside stood chairs, a canvas hung in front of them, and when we were all seated, the light was extinguished, a piano and violin began playing, and we saw "Judith and Holofernes," an historical drama in color. Thunderstruck, we looked at one another. The people painted in the picture moved, and the branches of the painted trees stirred.

In the morning, when I was settling down to write to Serge about Judith, Evgenia came in and handed me a note, rolled up into a tube. "How did you like the living photography?" was written in it. "I was sitting behind you. Let's you and I get acquainted. S."

The authoress of this letter awaited an answer, seated on the bench in front of the house, and when I came out of the gates, she rose. —I'm Stephania Grikyupel—she gave her name, and we went for a stroll. We admired the copper pretzel over the bakery door and the sugar Polish church. —My friend Serge went away to Yalta—I told her—and Andrey Kondratyev is at the encampments. I could go visit there, but Andrey doesn't really suit me, because he takes it upon himself to pronounce on everything. Stephania Grikyupel, it turned out, was also entering school and was terribly scared that it would be difficult for her: numerals in Arabic and composing compositions.

Pleased with one another, we parted. Approaching my gate I saw a funeral—torchbearers in loose white overalls, a hearse with a dome, adorned with a crown, and the widow behind the hearse. She was being led by Vasya Strizhkin.

I really caught it from maman when she returned. She forbade me meetings with Stephania and called Stephania depraved. Chigildeeva, who came to listen, stood up for me. —But it's so natural—she said and fell to thinking about something. Smiling, she scrambled upstairs and got "Favor for Favor." —I'm giving it to you—she told me.

12

The school was brown, and its facade, divided into segments by gutters, reminded you of chocolate. Affixed to the little pediment's triangular field was a cast-iron eagle. With one claw it gripped a snake, and in the other held a scepter. At the end where the church was situated, there was a cross on the roof.

I didn't have much luck in arithmetic, and I looked for encounters with Vasya Strizhkin. Often I waited for him around the coat stands or climbed up to the senior pupils' corridor. There opposite the stairs was a clock. On either side of it hung paintings: "The Baptism of Kiev" and "The Miracle at the Borki Trainwreck."* Under the clock there was a red copper water barrel and a mug on an iron chain. The supervisor Ivan Moiseich would come rushing over to make me clear off. During the big recess Madame Golovnyova sold rolls and tea in the gymnastics hall. She was a sumptuous woman, a Pole, and Ivan Moiseich paid her court. Her husband Golovnyov, the janitor, squattish, would watch them, standing by the stove. I stood next to him, and all the customers were visible to me. But even there I didn't encounter Vasya.

Budrikh, Karl, was the brother of Elsa Budrikh. He lived near the Protestant church, and we walked home together. He told me about how, apparently, he once saw a gentleman and a lady turn into the old cemetery and, probably, do stupidities. I visited there. Burdocks blossomed amid the graves. A stone angel held a lyre in its hand. Carts rumbled in the distance. There were still no gentlemen or ladies, and I sat down on a tombstone to wait for them.

"State"—old fashioned letters were chiseled on it—"Councillors Pyotr Petrovich and Sofia Grigoryevna Schukin." I pictured them to myself.

No one ever came, so I stood up and, brushing myself off, left. Houses' chimneys and treetops with leaves that had turned colors were illumined by the sun. In a tavern, over the door to which a fish had been drawn, a little box played music. Clusters of rowanberries shown red over a greenish fence, alluring. "Monuments"—I noticed a sign painted gold—"of all creeds. Prauda." I recalled I. Stupel, the madonna in her establishment, and Tusenka.

Soon after, Kondratyeva visited us and invited us to a name-day party. —We now have a gramophone—she said to us. And we told her about the living photography. There were many guests at her name-day party. The gramophone sang funny songs. Everyone liked the joke about the Jewish boy a lot, and they repeated it. —But it's a pity—said one guest—that science invented it so late: otherwise we would now be able to hear the voice of Jesus Christ, delivering sermons. I was moved. Andrey winked at me and we went out into the "drawing room." Once again I saw "Zarathustra" and "Reval" on the table. Andrey, while talking, drew a little picture in the margins of "Zarathustra." "Facial"—he wrote a title beneath it—"Features."

On a Saturday once, when I had dined and was reading "The Stock Exchange News" by the window, Chaplinsky suddenly appeared outside it. He handed me two little melons and announced that the Karmanovs had arrived. I hurried off with him. I talked with him on the way. I asked him if he were glad of his masters' return, and learned that while they were away he had been working at the depot, where he was listed, although he was attached to Karmanov.

Serge was amiable. —It's nice—he said to me—being acquainted with a schoolboy. The engineer's missus hastily gave us tea and
ran off to see Sophie. We remained the two of us together, giggled a
while, and then fell silent and listened to the bell. Serge told me that
Tusenka, too, had arrived from the dacha. —She—he laughed—
thought that your surname was Yat.* It turned out there's a book
"Chekhov," in which telegraphists are hauled over the coals, and
there's such a name there.

The engineer arrived. He switched on the electric light, which
had been conducted to their place from the railroad, and I turned
away so as not to ruin my eyes. He sat down with us and we chatted
with him a while. —Imagine—I said—the schoolboys write bad
words on their school desks. —Body parts?—asked Serge, perking
up. I thought about Andrey with the "Facial Features" and about
how it was reprehensible to think about others in the presence of a
friend.

On Sunday we were in the firemen's park. Bold waltzes rang
out, and the firemen raced one another jumping in sacks. The children were given paper flags and formed into a line. Like soldiers,
Serge and I began to step in file. As from a train window we could
see the trees to the side of the square and the leaves that fell from
them. The engineer commended us. —The marching went off very
nicely—he said. While leaving we lingered and watched the policemen who had driven off idlers. —Yes—Serge pushed me and whispered that he'd found out for me from Sophie about Vasya
Strizhkin. In the summer his father had died, and he serves in the
police.

13

—"Orthodox"—Father Nikolay told us during "Scripture" lesson—means "correctly believing." On the way home from school I reported this to Budrikh. I set about persuading him to cross over to Orthodoxy, and he began avoiding me. So that when Serge asked me one day if I hadn't struck up a friendship at school, I was able to answer—no. Assuring him of this, I presented the pupils to him in an unattractive light. —They always have dirty nails—I said—and they don't clean their teeth. They say "ain't," "I could care less," "different from," and "the reason why." —Idiots—we laughed and put ourselves in an agreeable mood. The inscription on a box of cookies at tea reminded us of Tusenka. We winked at each other and, just like a verse, repeated all evening:

Siou and company, Moscow.
Siou and company, Moscow.

A few days later I met her in the school church. Rays stretched from the windows, dust revolved on them. Time just barely crawled. At last Golovnyov came out from behind the altar with the teapot and went to get the boiling water for communion. I looked back to follow him with my eyes, and saw her. After church I couldn't run after her and watch her from afar because Ivan Moiseich took us to the inspector for roll call.

Sophie's husband, the inspector, was transferred to Libau, and Sophie was leaving with him. On a cloudy day, just before evening, when, awaiting a lamp, I stopped learning what addition was for a minute, she knocked on our door to say good-bye. Cumbersome, wearing a hat with a plume and a veil with dots, she was melancholy. Maman told her that Evgenia was really too ingratiating. Therefore she didn't inspire trust, and we were thinking of sacking her. Upon parting, Sophie gave me a book about Mowgli,* which I really liked. I read it through several times. Chigildeeva, dropping in on us, would sneak up and try to see whether it were not "Favor for Favor" I was reading.

—Today—announced Karmanova once, when I was staring out the window with Serge—is going to be "Fright Night"*—and she advised us to go to the river and watch the Jews throng there to shake off their sins. Under Chaplinsky's protection we ran to the river. We laughed terribly. Chaplinsky told us that every spring little Christian boys vanish, and taught us how to show a "pig's ear."*

It was already just beginning to freeze. Maman, whenever going outdoors, was already putting on woolen pantaloons. Chigildeeva sealed up her mezzanine and left for Yaroslavl to be godmother at her niece's. She died there. She left me three hundred rubles, and maman told me not to spread this fact around.

Winter came. It was Saturday evening. The moon shone, and the gilt hands of the clock on the Protestant church glittered. From the viaduct I saw lights on the tracks and a sheaf of sparks over the baths. A cabby's sleigh sped past. Sitting in it was Vasya Strizhkin, wearing an officer's-colored overcoat. Bells clattered. For several days I waited for the good fortune this encounter was supposed to bring me. And, indeed, one morning when we arrived at school the janitor told us that Father Nikolay had fallen ill, and that day we had four lessons.

A "Play for Children," posters proclaimed one day. I pictured a beautiful maiden, prostrating herself before an imposing youth and exclaiming: —Oh, Alexander! Chaplinsky brought us tickets. The theater was full. The military orchestra under the direction of Kapellmeister Schmidt rang out. Before us was the curtain with the castle. We waited for it to rise, and chewed candies. Stephania Grikyupel sprang out from somewhere and, before I turned, managed to nod to me. I was glad that maman and the Karmanovs were at that moment watching Madame Strauss enter the hall.

Christmas flew past, and one day in a special edition of the newspaper "Dvina" it was announced that Japan had attacked us. Church services began to stretch even longer. Mass would end, and a prayer service "for the granting of victory" would begin. In L. Kusman's window "patriotic letters" appeared. Serge began to cut out photographs of battleships and cruisers from the "New Times" and paste them into a "scratch-book." Once Maman and I were at the Karmanovs. The ladies had conversed about the fact that lint* is no longer used now in war and distinguished ladies no longer gather together to prepare it.

That evening Tusenka came to the Karmanovs with her mother. Serge chatted with her a bit and ran off to his room to get the "scratch-book." I and Tusenka were alone together at the end of the "hall." Sophie and her friends had performed an interesting drama here once, one scene of which I had spied on. I wanted to recount it to Tusenka. —Nathalie, ah—I wanted to say to her. We both were silent, and already I heard Serge returning. —Have you read the book "Chekhov"?—she finally asked, reddening.

14

The first week of Lent our school fasted. Maman explained to me how it was sinful to conceal anything during confession. I didn't know what to do because it seemed to me that it wouldn't be very comfortable confessing sins to Father Nikolay. Therefore, I was very glad when he told us that he wasn't going to lose much time with the preparatory-class kids, and gathering us under a black apron which he raised up over us, ordered us all at one go to confess our sins mentally.

Spring came quickly. On the Sunday before Holy Week an edifying reading took place at the school. I was there with maman.

There was a magic lantern, and Father Nikolay, enclosed by a screen, read about the last days in the life of Jesus Christ. Illumined by a candle, he was visible through the chintz. When we were heading toward the exit, someone called to us. We turned. Gorshkova nodded to us and signaled. With a lorgnette and wearing a boa, she was very impressive. She questioned me about my progress and said that she would now be living closer to us, because she had changed parishes. While conversing, she held me by the chin.

We were remembered in Vitebsk by the lady who came when Father died. On a postcard with a picture called "Noli me tangere,"* she wished us a happy Easter and informed us that her daughter had gotten married to a gentleman of German background, a landowner, and that they were going away to the estate and she herself was planning to move with them too.

Examinations were already beginning. It was a bright evening. Trees were blossoming. Sitting in the garden, I was reviewing about addition. A window opened and maman called me into the house and told me to say good-bye to Alexandra Lvovna, who was setting off for the Far East. She was in a "nurse" uniform, hurrying and drinking, pouring into two saucers: —Let it cool off more quickly. —You'll conquer them—maman was saying—and then our tea will be inexpensive.

For the summer the Karmanovs moved to Shavskie Drozhki, and after examinations maman and I visited with them. From the steamship "Progress" we could see the dike and the fortress. The orchestra that had embarked upon the steamship together with us was playing. Whenever it fell silent, the people near us would discuss England and condemn her. —A Christian nation—they would say— and she's helping the Japanese. —Indeed—shrugging her shoulders, maman turned to me with astonishment. I was confused. It was printed on the book about Mowgli that it was a translation from the English, and therefore I had thought one had to love England.

The engineer's missus and Serge came out to meet us. Festive, we walked through the park. Seated on a stage, our orchestra had already begun ringing out. Ladies in corsets, wearing sashes with bugles and stiff coiffures with a roller set beneath the hair, rose from the benches and set off along the paths. Men with beards and mustaches, wearing white regimental tunics, escorted them. Serge bowed to one of the women and informed me that it was—the notary Konrad von Sassaparel's missus. Balloons on green pedestals and verandas with sailcloth festoons stood out vividly behind little fences. Knives banged in kitchens. Dacha ladies luxuriated in hammocks under trees. Running and arguing with one another, young ladies and little boys played croquet.

While parting, the Karmanovs asked maman to stop by their city apartment sometimes to be sure that Chaplinsky was guarding it carefully. That very evening we called in there. We found Chaplinsky asleep. Throwing on his overcoat, he let us in, and we went around to all the rooms with him. He called us to the window and, important, pointed to the garden. Beneath the chestnut trees, where the nannies had always sung, were sitting the basement people. —They're taking advantage—he explained to us gloomily—of the ladies' and gentlemen's departure. We told the Karmanovs of this, and they wrote to Kantorek for him to take measures.

I did not remain with nothing to do for long. Maman made arrangements with Gorshkova, and I began going to her to study German, so that I'd already know something for the start of studies in school. "*Was ist das?*" Gorshkova would dictate and, while I wrote, would approach me. I'd hide my hands, and she wouldn't be able to grab them. Lost in thought, she'd sometimes start looking at me. Once in the anteroom she told me that Pleve[*] had been killed, and, upset, attacking quickly, she grabbed me and squeezed.

Now and then I'd come upon Stephania. Bowing to her, I'd assume a stern air and she wouldn't dare to start talking with me.

15

—Prayer service tomorrow at school—announced maman one day and handed me the "Dvina." I read the notice. —So—thought I—summer's already at an end. For the last time I went to Shavskie Drozhki. On the vines there the leaves had already thinned out. Gossamer already was flying. At the Karmanovs I saw Sophie. She was stopping there in passing with her little child. Clumsy, rising from the rocking chair, she inspected me. —Still the same as always—she said showily—but there's already something different in the eyes. Konrad von Sassaparel's missus called while I was there. Imposing, she leaned on a staff. On it there were horns and the inscription "Crimée." The engineer's missus sat down near her and they were saying that they should get Samokvasovo off their hands quickly, and that in general it would be good to sell off everything and move. I was alarmed. —Serge will go away too—I thought—and that will be the end of friendship. Sad, I returned home on the "Progress." Its two wheels made noise. The passengers were silent. On a little hill a garden was visible, and through the little garden a sunset could be seen.

This year as a book supplement L. Kusman gave me "The Thoughts of Wise People." On their cover it was written that they cost twelve kopecks. Maman looked through them and approved a couple, and I was glad. But at school I found out that Yampolsky and Livshitz were giving out "Comrade: A Calendar for Schoolboys." Disappointed, I resolved never more to have anything to do with L. Kusman. I was thinking about this when I went out in the evening to take a stroll. Preoccupied, I didn't notice the penmanship teacher on the street, and for this I was put in the punishment room for an hour. I sobbed all that day, and maman brought me drops.

Now the secondary-school girls were being brought to our

church. They wore white pinafores, little bows, and, without turning their heads, watched us out of the corners of their eyes. Their headmistress, wearing a "ribbon," solemn, would sometimes take a handkerchief from her little bag, and then the smell of violet would waft over to us. Tusenka stood in file decorously, pretending that she didn't notice anything around her, and reddened when anyone looked at her. —Nathalie, Nathalie—I'd think, and masses no longer seemed to me so long.

In class I sat next to Friedrich Olov. He was a bad student and during lessons, tearing out a sheet from the copybook, he loved to draw stupidities on it. He assured me that everything they said about Podolskaya Street was the truth, and I, returning from school, several times made a detour and walked along Podolskaya, but I didn't see anything remarkable on it. One time I ran into the Osip who had once studied with me at Gorshkova's there, and he had a good laugh over having encountered me there. He was a ragamuffin, and it occurred to me later that he might have a knife and that he could help me take revenge on the penmanship teacher. After considering how I was to talk with him, I went to see him at the school in which he used to live, but he was no longer there.

That fall we moved to a different apartment. It was on the same block, in Kanatchikov's stone house. Coming for the money, Kanatchikov would start up a conversation about religion. He would show us how you were supposed to cross yourself with two fingers.* From our house we now could see the square on which they trained soldiers. Situated in a corner of it, surrounded by yellow acacia, was a little military church. Standing by the window, we'd hear the prayer service conducted on the square whenever regiments were sent to war.

The Karmanovs were at our housewarming. They hadn't moved away. An inexpensive place had turned up for them not far from Evpatoria, and they were planning to build an income cottage there.

Along with two of the Pferdchens Serge had already begun studying at Gausmansha's to enter the first form in the spring. Serge told
me that Gausmansha said "five fives." After laughing at this, we
chatted together pleasantly in my room and didn't turn on the light.
The siren in the factory shops hooted. There was soft ringing in the
bell tower on the square. Sometimes whistles reached us from the
tracks. We put ourselves in a serious mood. I related something
from "History," and we marveled at the Slavs who had put straws
in their mouths for breathing and sat all day under water. Taking
leave of our guests, I listened from the porch to their steps rustling
on the sand. I stood like Manilov. A star fell and I was sorry that at
that moment I hadn't been thinking about revenge on the teacher—
or else it would have turned out as I had wished.

16

—You've got to eat more rice—maman now said at dinner—and
then you'll be strong. The Japanese eat only rice—and look how
they're defeating us.

Just as every year, we were again at the Kondratyevs' name-day
party. Kondratyeva read us several letters from her husband. I really liked in them the words "*kauliang*" and "*fan-jiao*."* Andrey, too,
like Serge, was planning to enter the first form. He was preparing
with the teacher Tevel Lvovich.

All the guys were busy now, and I saw them rarely. I practically
didn't meet with Serge at all. Karmanova, however, visited us very
often. She liked the church opposite our house. The priest there
now was a monk. He wore a black cowl from which something hung
down in back, and a mantle. It made one curious.

The penmanship teacher was absent for several days. He was
sick. I wished him death and prayed that God would put him in hell.

But he soon turned up. "Judas"—he wrote out painstakingly on the board—"betrayed Jesus Christ with a kiss"—and we began to copy.

At Christmas I went almost nowhere. The Karmanovs rolled off to Libau to visit Sophie and sent from there a little postcard of a Protestant church and the inscription "*Frohliche Weihnachten.*"

This year the engineer's missus fell in love with politics. She'd often begin expatiating on them, and then maman's and my eyes would start to stick together.

It had begun dripping from the roofs whenever the sun came out, and I grew more and more tired of school. I was very glad when one sunny morning, important, Golovnyov announced to us by the cloakroom that some prince had been killed and that at twelve o'clock we would depart for the requiem, and from there—home. He loved to announce the unexpected.

I left the requiem solemn. Olov suggested that we go to the market. I had never yet been there, and off we ran. We giggled and, holding on to one another, shoved. Cooks nearly knocked us over, grazing us with their baskets. Ladies, stopping by the cartloads of food, were sampling. Peasants were saying foul things out loud. I was seeing them up close for the first time. —They're like beasts— said Olov, and we had a chat about them.

The time for fasting and confession drew near, but I didn't think about it much. I had already decided that I wasn't confessing anything to Father Nikolay, because he could snitch or play dirty tricks himself.

That lady who had once come to us from Vitebsk again sent a postcard. She invited us to come stay with her. We made up our minds, and maman wrote an application for vacation.

Summer finally arrived. We parted with the Karmanovs, who went off to build the cottage, and set off on our trip as well. We asked Kanatchikov to keep an eye on Evgenia.

A carriage met us by the railroad. With great interest we rose from our seats and looked when the estate came into view up ahead. The smokestack of a distillery stood over it. Peasants were harrowing. Ravens revolved about them. I pictured to myself Chichikov's travels.

We presented ourselves and they began questioning us. We recalled a little of our conversations with Karmanova. —The common people are rebelling—we said. —Measures that can be taken are few.

Toward evening we went to watch the workers dancing on the other side of the park on a floor encircled with benches. This floor had been laid specially for them, so that they wouldn't loaf around in their free time and were always within eyeshot.

Upon returning, we sat a while on the porch steps, like "Gogol in Vasilevka."* A bird suddenly trilled and whistled. —Quiet— said maman. She raised a finger to her lips and looked at us with a blissful face. —Nightingale—she whispered.

I was forbidden to go beyond the gate, and I didn't aspire to. It would have been terrifying suddenly to encounter peasants alone. From the room called the "library" I extracted "Arabian Tales for Adults" and read them in the garden during our stay. "Stupidities" had been written about in them. I was now convinced that the boys hadn't been lying.

On St. John's Eve Letts* came to the house with fires and branches and put garlands on us all. For a long time they skipped and sang and burned barrels of tar. We treated them to beer and went to bed when everyone had gone away and the fires had been doused and the gates had been shut and the watchman had begun to knock, as always, with a board.

They'd already written a request for soldiers to protect the estate. Soon, standing at the windows, we saw them enter the yard. They were unprepossessing, but stocky, carried rifles, and sang about Stessel:*

General Stessel, though not defeated,
Reports his shells are soon depleted.

17

Once more I landed at Gorshkova's for instruction. When we arrived back in town, maman sent me to learn a little French. —It's a difficult language—Gorshkova would say. —All the letters in it are written like this but are read like that. Wishing to encourage me, she would aim to catch hold of my hands to squeeze them, but I'd manage to jerk them away and quickly sit on them. I didn't like Gorshkova very much. Her skin reminded me of the bottom crust of a loaf of bread, farinaceous and rough.

It was a hot day. The sun wasn't visible. Gardens smelled of apples. On the road to Gorshkova's I met a little boy with the "Dvina." —Peace Resolution!—he was yelling. I asked him if it were true, and he showed me the headline.

Gorshkova didn't know anything about the peace yet, and I didn't tell her so she wouldn't get all emotional and go for me and knead me.

We were very glad about the peace, but Karmanova, returning from Evpatoria, dampened our ardor. —If we'd fought a bit longer—she told us—we'd have won. Witte* concocted all this on purpose, because he's married to a Jew, and she's been egging him on.

Serge let me look at the "dacha model"—it was made of wood, with real glass in the windows. They were painting the school, and the beginning of classes had been postponed for two weeks, but he was already strutting around in uniform.

This year I purchased textbooks from Yampolsky. I finally

received a "Calendar." I wouldn't walk past L. Kusman now. She might suddenly open the door and, holding her kerchief to her breasts, look at me and ask why it was I hadn't come to her for books till now.

Serge and Andrey were now both in the first form. Serge was in "basic," and Andrey in "parallel." They had "Scripture" lessons in common, and then they'd sit together. Once Andrey drew a little picture during "Scripture." "Please come to table," it was titled, "my dear guests." Karmanova, upon seeing it, was very displeased. —It's always some sort of libel—she started to say with disgust. —Before you criticize, you've got to be perfect yourself. She ordered Serge to change seats.

We had already celebrated the heir to the throne's name day and stood through the service marking the anniversary of the "salvation at Borki." The next day, after they'd rung the bells and the teacher had entered, stroking his beard, and then, crossing himself, had taken his place by the icon, and the student on duty had begun to read "Most Blessed," a bomb suddenly exploded with a terrible crash somewhere nearby. They closed the school that day for an indefinite period.

When we were having dinner, the sirens in the factory shops suddenly began hooting in a peculiar way. Later we heard shots. Toward night Evgenia found out for us that four people had been shot. The rebels had picked them up and were carrying them by torchlight through the streets to stir up the people.

We watched as they were buried. Polish priests with pompous faces strutted up front. —What scoundrels—Karmanova said and explained to us that, according to their religion, they're supposed to be for the government, but they hate Russia and are prepared for anything as long as it does us dirty. Orchestras from the factory shops and fire brigades were playing behind the graves. For almost an entire hour, long ago having ceased to interest us, flags and sheets with legends on them moved past our windows, tottering. We learned that later there had been an exchange of gunfire near the cemetery, during which Vasya Strizhkin had been wounded by shot. Poor fellow, until it healed he could neither sit nor lie on his back.

So that I wouldn't be loafing about, maman told me to read "The Works of Turgenev." I read them diligently, but they didn't particularly interest me.

Time and again we'd begin going to school and then quit anew. We began using the words "mass meeting," "Black Hundreds,"* "orange," "snitch." One day, when we were out on strike once again, Serge and Andrey stopped by to see me and told me how just now they'd broken up the German school. They had seized the class journal in it. The "alphabet" began: "Anokhina, Boldyreva." I laughed, but toward evening began to feel sad. I thought about how everyone was doing something interesting except me, but still I couldn't come up with anything.

At maman's there were also sometimes strikes. She was on the "right," but readily went on strike. She told me once that her chief had been at a "mass meeting" and had resolved never to go again because, while he was there, he felt that he agreed with the impermissible arguments. We praised him.

Both Yampolsky and Lifshitz were giving out with each purchase little coupons with a designation of the purchase sum, and whoever presented ten rubles' worth of these—would receive something. The pupil Martinkevich, through whom his father purchased office supplies, received from Yampolsky an album for writing verses in. When we were studying at school he'd demand that you write him something. I held on to this little album for a long time and was tormented because I didn't know what to write. I found some verses in it called "A Decoction of Salvation." They began:

Procure an ounce of humbleness,
Add two of patient sufferance—

and were signed: "With the blessings of Father Gavriil." It turned out that the monk from the church opposite our house was Martinkevich's relative.

18

I wanted to find out from the monk if God would agree to put someone in hell if you were to pray for this well and truly, and in order to meet the monk I planned to take up with Martinkevich. I didn't manage to, because our regiments returned and those who were replacing them left, and the monk left with them.

From Asia the officers brought lots of all sorts of bric-a-brac. Kondratyev presented us with little knickknacks to hang on the wall. Where once "Zarathustra" had lain on his table, now "The Red Laugh"* appeared. He let us read it.

Soon after we saw Alexandra Lvovna as well. She had aged. She informed us that she had dedicated herself to the care of Doctor Vagel, who had been contused in the head, and she hinted that, perhaps, she wouldn't be parting from him in any case. We became pleasantly pensive.

It turned out that the church to which Karmanova so gladly had gone when the monk was here could be dismantled. It was unscrewed and dispatched to the suburbs of Kreuzberg, where part of the Letts were Orthodox. Now in its place a "garrison cathedral" was supposed to be built. We anticipated with interest just what it would be like.

One bright evening, when I and maman were drinking tea, Chaplinsky reported to us. With great animation he announced that someone had shot at Karmanov on his way home from the office, and that a quarter of an hour later he had died.

Curious women began coming to see us and question us about the Karmanovs. We answered them. Regarding the engineer's missus maman told them that she had not been living with the engineer for several years already. I was astonished and corrected her, but she told me not to interfere in grown-ups' conversations.

Suddenly I caught a cold in my throat, and it so happened I wasn't at the funeral. I watched it from the window. Wearing a "submarine" hat that had already gone out of fashion after the war's conclusion, maman walked with Karmanova. They screened Serge from me. But I did find Tusenka in the crowd. It seemed to me that she imperceptibly threw me a glance.

Serge told me later that he had taken an oath to avenge his father. I squeezed his hand and didn't tell him that avenging was very difficult.

Soon I was supposed to part with him. He was going away forever. The engineer's missus had already been to Moscow and found an apartment. The departure had been postponed until the beginning of school vacation. Loneliness awaited me.

They started building the cathedral. They dug the earth. They carted cobblestone. On the block behind the Protestant church they began building a Polish church. The Old Believers attached a bell tower to their "prayer house." Father Nikolay explained to us that all creeds had been granted freedom, but that didn't really have much significance and, as before, the principal religion would remain ours.

The Karmanovs seated themselves in the carriage. The train started. We waved to it. —Serge, Serge, ah, Serge—I didn't manage to say—Serge, will you remember me as I'll remember you?

The Belugins came to Shavskie Drozhki from Mitau for the summer. We visited them. It was strange for me to see the *kursaal*, the park, and know that I'd meet Serge here no more. Maman was also sad.

At the Belugins we found Siou, Tusenka's father. He had a small beard and wore glasses. He looked like the portrait of Petrunkevich.* —Have you read Muromtsev's* speech?—he graciously asked maman.

The Belugins' daughter and son were a little younger than I. I began going to visit them in Shavskie Drozhki. Belugina was a lean woman with a lorgnette and pockmarks. She spent her time beneath the pines, rocking in a hammock and reading the newspaper. Belugin, her husband, fished. Her sister, Olga Kuskova, would take us to the woods. Once we went as far as the railroad and saw a train carrying soldiers. It was rolling toward Kreuzberg. Officers looked out at us from the passenger carriages. —"Punitives"—Olga Kuskova explained to us.

Sometimes Tusenka would drop in on the Belugins while I was there, but she put on airs with me and addressed me formally.

When I wasn't there, I was reading Dostoevsky. He astounded me, and maman would say at dinner that I acted as if I'd been—scalded.

The days passed. Sandy shoals already had appeared on the river, and the "Progress" maneuvered to keep from running aground on them. In a little black frame the newspaper "Dvina" printed the untimely death of the penmanship teacher.

Once I came across Osip. He was amiable. He offered to show where the hanged men were buried. I recounted to him the incident with the teacher. —Osip—I said—would you have agreed to kill him if he hadn't died himself? I took his hand and, excited, looked at him. He answered me that for an acquaintance everything would be possible. I was sorry that I'd met him so late.

19

Once again autumn was just around the corner. In the front garden acacia pods already crackled as they split. In times of rain, when the dust was beaten down, the basement people would open their windows. Then we'd hurry to shut our windows so that the stench wouldn't burst in upon us. —Before—maman would say—you simply could have sent Evgenia down and forbid them.

I no longer found Friedrich Olov at school. He'd been taken to Riga in the summer and employed in the trading house of "Knie, Falk and Fyodorov." Entering in place of him was a new boy by the name of Sofronychev. He was called "Gregoire." He was the son of the chief of police, transferred to us to replace Lomov. Tusenka made friends with Gregoire's sister "Agatha" and went with her to the theater and the circus for free. I could have seen her often if I'd joined Gregoire's coterie of friends. But he was a slob, and, moreover, over the course of the last year I had grown used to not liking policemen.

One holiday Andrey called on me. He looked through my "Scripture" textbook and, chuckling over the "chasuble" illustration, suggested I go for a stroll with him.

Maman was at the telegraph, and I left with Andrey without permission. I wasn't sure whether I'd done the right thing in going off with him. We examined building sites. A Jewess wearing a fringed shawl approached us. —Don't—she said—beat that boy wearing the gray stockings. We laughed. Then we listened to a man in suspenders, who was sitting by a gate, play a horn.

"Chalk, screws,"
was listed on a board fastened to the gate,
"brushes, nails and glues,"
and, lost in thought, we sang these words to the sounds of the horn.

While conversing, we found ourselves near the cemetery. Sunset was already reflected in the letters over the entrance. The flowers on the graves were in their last bloom. Trees were shedding their leaves. Ungainly angels, standing with one leg on a pedestal, looked up at the sky as if getting ready to fly. Favorably disposed, I was already beginning to tell myself that, all the same, Andrey too was nice. And suddenly, near the little column with the urn over Karmanov's remains, he began talking all sorts of nonsense. —He wouldn't have been killed—he said, by the way—without some reason. Indignant, I tried not to listen to him and repented of having agreed to come.

I decided that it would be best for me not to see him at all. But once again we were invited to the Kondratyevs' name day, and maman brought me. The guests were seated along the walls. Portrayed in the pictures were a mountain with a Japanese woman at its foot, bending over a bench that had grub on it. I sat down behind maman. They were saying that when the current is turned on there's going to be an electric theater working here. Andrey, as always, directed me with a wink toward the doors of the "drawing-room," and I pretended I didn't understand. But soon maman ordered me not to sit with the adults. I was forced to agree to go into the garden.

We noticed several apples and knocked them down. We busied ourselves with them, sitting on the steps. Chewing, we tried to imagine the electric theater. It was doubtless bound to be unusually beautiful. —Andrey—I said, moving closer—there's a certain schoolgirl by the name of Tusenka. —Susenka?—he asked back. I got up and left him. While going to sleep that evening I thought that "Tusenka," it's true, is sort of a stupid name, and that it would be best to call her thus: Nathalie.

After mass on Sunday I went down behind the dike. There I took a look at the electric station's scaffolding and wandered around a bit. The kitchen gardens, already empty, began beyond the last little shop, and in that shop's windows, just as long, long ago, I saw the hanging candles. The old lady made of cotton, smoke-cured through and through like a chimney sweep, was here too. Dead flies stuck to her. The cranberries in the little basket behind her back gleamed white. A pleasant sadness gripped me, and I was glad that, just like an adult, I was already "reminded of childhood."

One day maman met Alexandra Lvovna at the baths. She had gotten married to Doctor Vagel. He—she recounted—hasn't completely cured his head yet and sometimes displays various oddities. They hadn't celebrated their wedding. They'd gotten married quietly in Griva-Zemgalskaya.

Pleased, we had a good laugh.

Sofronychev "fugued" for several days: he'd leave home in the morning and wouldn't appear at school. It became known that the literature teacher had visited the chief of police. Together they'd given Gregoire a sound flogging with a rope. I thought that perhaps after this Nathalie would be ashamed to sit with him in the chief of police's box at the theater.

20

"Serge," I wrote during lessons on sheets torn from a notebook, "I've noticed that I'm already becoming like a grown-up. Sometimes I'm already reminded of childhood. It seems to me that others also find this so. Evgenia, our cook, for example, when maman isn't there, more and more readily turns up in rooms to discuss things with me." I wrote how she would tell me about Kanatchikov, how his son sits chained under his house, and how this son is stupid, or about basement Annushka—how she accompanies the troops on maneuvers and sells them provisions, and how when maneuvers are over she still somehow or other earns money from the troops, but Kanatchikov picks on her and curses her if people come to see her at home.

"Serge," I wrote, "you know I'm scribbling this to you during arithmetic. It makes no difference, I have no luck at it anyway. I wonder if it isn't because I can't, for some reason, make out the smaller figures on the board. Therefore I can't manage to follow the lesson.

"I read a lot. I've already read through "Dostoevsky" twice. What I like about him, Serge, is that there's a lot that's funny.

"Have you heard, Serge, that apparently Chichikov and all the inhabitants of the town of N, and Manilov as well, are—scoundrels? We're taught this in school. I had a good laugh over this.

"Serge, what would you say about a person who a) puts on airs b) goes to the theater without paying, through patronage?"

I would tear up my letters when they were ready, and throw the scraps behind the cupboard, because I had no money for stamps, and maman would have read them before sending them.

"Serge," I wrote further, "have you ever seen wrestlers? I wouldn't mind having a look at them, Serge, but, you know, maman heard somewhere that it's—crude."

At Yuletide a "students' ball" took place on the school's premises. In the gymnastics hall, filled with Christmas trees, a great many lamps had been lit. The military orchestra had been arranged between the stoves, and was playing under the direction of Kapellmeister Schmidt. Madame Strauss felt like listening a bit closer, and she walked up to the stoves and stood attentive, holding in her hands the sugar bowl she had won in the "lottery allegri."*

Actors from the theater came out onto the stage and recited verses. Madmazelle Evstigneeva sang. Schukina, proprietress of Musical Education for Everyone, played, shaking the feather adorning her head. Perhaps, I thought, she's the daughter of those "State Councillors Schukin" whose grave I once sat on while waiting for the "gentlemen and ladies."

They announced an intermission for the opening of windows and the removal of chairs. Among those bustling about was Lieberman. He looked very smart in uniform with a sword and a "managerial armband." I recalled Sophie, his coeval, who had once acted so successfully with him in a drama, and I became sad: poor thing, somehow she already seemed twenty years older than he.

Waltzers had already begun twirling in the cleared area. Karl Pferdchen whirled with his sister Edith. Konrad von Sassaparel's missus stepped forward with Bodrevich, publisher of the newspaper "Dvina." Nathalie, blushing, accepted the invitation of Gregoire, who had come running up to her. The literature teacher, past whom I was walking, winked at him. He smiled, flattered. I was given a letter from "Cupid's courier." "Why is it," someone was asking me in it, "you're pensive?" Curiosity excited, I began looking at all the faces and, like Chichikov, tried to guess who had written. While doing this I caught sight of L. Kusman and hastened to escape.

I didn't return home right away, but strolled along the dike. Dreamy, I'd pull the note I'd received at the ball from my pocket and then hide it again. The weather was changing from thaw to slight frost, and before my eyes the clouds crawled away and a dark sky with stars opened up. Two sleighs passed me unhurriedly. —You got any tobacco?—the peasant in the rear asked the one up front. I was a bit surprised hearing peasants conversing, just like we do.

I saved the little letter, and considered poetic the minutes I'd now and then spend reading it.

Spring approached. From the Karmanovs I received a proposal that I spend the summer with them. They promised to come get me. Maman made me striped trunks.

That winter we saw a member of the State Duma.* Kanatchikov was making an inspection of what repairs were required. He was standing by the window and feeling the frames. The Duma member suddenly drove past—in a little sleigh, harnessed with a big gray horse under olive-green netting. Kanatchikov called to us. We ran up and managed to catch a glimpse of dashing cheek and black beard. —Ours, extreme right—Kanatchikov told us. We smiled pleasantly.

21

Karmanova still had some little business affairs in our town. She was selling a plot that had come her way through a mortgage. Because of this she stayed with us for several days.

I and Serge were together a while in Shavskie Drozhki. The orchestra played, as always. Splashes could be heard from the bathhouses. The vine over the river was blossoming. —Serge, you remember—I said—once we were happy here.

We traveled in the train for a long time. In the morning we'd jump up to see the sunrise. Toward the end of the day the clouds took on the appearance of mountains surrounding the water.

Arriving in Sebastopol we hastily examined the cathedral and the panorama,* and before evening sailed away. En route we fell ill with seasickness. We arrived late, and in the dark I could see neither the mosque nor the church. I had long known them from the postcard "Greetings from Evpatoria."

We were boarded onto launches. I became faint as I climbed down the rope ladder. —Vasenka—I screamed in my mind. Someone caught me from below.

Karaat, harnessed to a wagonette, awaited us by the pier. He had been rented from Tatars for the summer. Holding the reins, the driver—at the "dacha" he was manager, coachman, gardener, and watchman—turned to Karmanova and began to make her a report.

Identical, one after the other the days went by. We'd rise. Karmanova, wearing a "red matiné made from shawls with a Turkish design," would begin scurrying between the "wing," in which we lived, and the "dacha." Bakers appeared with baskets. Karaat began carrying the summerfolk to the mudbaths and the city. Karmanova, in pince-nez, standing by the gate, marked in a little notebook who was going where. Gazing languidly, Alexander Khalkiopov, a student, would come out into the yard. We would greet him and head off with him toward the sea.

We spent the whole morning by the sea, lolling about, taking a handful of sand and slowly pouring it out, grain by grain. Alexander told us interesting things. There were often things I wouldn't understand. —You're a child—Serge would then say—click your heels for us. In Moscow he'd gotten to know a lot of new stuff, a lot of which I could never even have imagined.

After dinner, I'd go off with Serge into the shade. There he'd read "The Count of Monte Cristo" or "The Three Musketeers." He had borrowed them from the library. When he would finish reading the first book and start on the next, I'd begin to read the first. It was only the last book I didn't manage to get through; Serge returned it when he'd finished it. I then remembered about Chigildeeva's money. If I had already been able to dispose of it, I could have subscribed to the library myself and not have depended on anyone.

In the evening all the dacha ladies would call to one another and gather on the main terrace. Draped in "yashmaks" made of gauze and embroidered with spangles, they would lead Alexander off in a gang to stroll. Their husbands would set off for the billiard room. The children would sit down on the swing seat and quietly swing. I and Serge would come up and lean against the posts. It would get dark. The engineer's missus was reading "Quo Vadis?"* by lamp-light on her veranda. The cook and her helper, also with a little lamp, were sitting on the back porch, cleaning vegetables for the next day. A steamboat hooted at sea. Sometimes, not far away, a horn would begin to play.

"Chalk, screws,"

I'd then soundlessly join in,

"brushes, nails, and glues."

Approaching the gate, the wagonette rumbling, Karaat would come running in, and they'd unharness him.

In a cupboard I found a book called "The Life of Jesus."* It astonished me. I didn't think it possible to doubt in the divinity of Jesus Christ. Hiding, I read it through, and told no one I'd read it. —Whatever, then—I said to myself—can you be sure of completely?

New summer folk would right away go out and sit in the sun for hours, and it would scorch them. We'd advise them to use "Ideal," Petrova's cream. Then we'd go over to see her and receive a "commission." By this means I got to finish "Musketeers" and "Count" and also saved two twenty-kopeck pieces.

Soon watermelons and muskmelons made their appearance. Now Karaat was fed on their rinds. —If he doesn't eat them—said Karmanova—it means he's full up.

One Sunday Alexander decided to make a trip to town. He took us with him. On the boulevard we sat down. Absentminded, some girls ran past us. He stretched out his leg, and they tripped. Burying his face in his handkerchief, Serge laughed horribly. I thought about how he was already too enthralled with Alexander, and it began seeming to me that he was indifferent toward me.

The Karaite lady Turshu, our new summer resident, asked me one day to show her where the chiromancer lived. I walked with her along the stone walls behind which apricot trees, squattish, grew.

She was very brown, with darkened eyelids, and wore a pink dress and green "yashmak." —Let's have a little chat—she suggested to me, and I told her how the engineer had been killed. —Of course, he wouldn't have been killed—said I—without some reason.

I returned from Evpatoria alone. The engineer's missus gave me a "Perekop melon" for maman. Turshu waved after me from the window of her room, and Alexander, who stood together with her at the window, nodded to me. Serge got onto the wagonette with me and went for the drive to the steamship.

22

When I arrived and came out of the station onto the square, the city seemed strange to me. There were no trees to be seen on the streets. The cabbies were dressed for winter. Their droshkies had but a single horse. You didn't hear the sound of the sea. I pictured to myself the "Count's Pier"—columns and statues and steps down to the water. —Serge, Serge, ah, Serge—I sighed from habit.

The cathedral opposite our house was nearly completed. Its cupolas were hidden by canvas awnings that looked like tents. The cabby told me that up there were—gilders.

Annushka with her grandma and daughter Fedka was standing by the house in sunlight. Perhaps, I thought, looking at those tents she recalls maneuvers. She bowed and shouted something.

Maman was at home. Catching sight of me from the window, she ran out, and Evgenia ran out after her. They questioned me while I washed. —There you see—said maman—how nice it is to have acquaintances with means.

After finding out everything from me, she herself began informing me of what had happened over the course of the summer. That place where the exhibition had been situated, it turned out, was now called the "Nikolay Park." An outdoor party to benefit the "Russian Philanthropic Society" had been organized there. Schukina, sitting in a booth, had sold flowers, and maman had helped her: Mr. Siou had met and seated her.

She began looking at the window, beaming. I was agitated. On the very first day of arrival I had heard about Schukina, whose "Education" Nathalie visited on "odd-numbered days," and about Mister Siou. I thought that, perhaps, this was an—omen.

I went for a run. Here and there along the dike workmen were sitting, smashing cobblestones into road metal for highway repairs. They were already removing the planked footway and supports from the electric station. Master Jan Jutt had moved, together with his chemist's shop, to a new home of his own—it was decorated around the entrance with a bas-relief "owl."

I wandered a while between Schukina and Janek's house. If Nathalie were suddenly to appear here—well-mannered, with modest mien and "music" folder—I would say to her: —Hello.

Turning up among the repeaters in class were Sergei Mitrofanov from "Religious Objects" and—Schuster. He lived in our house, and we walked home together from school. He told me that his younger brother had been expelled because he'd already sat through the first form twice and had been left behind for a third year. Their father had thrashed him and handed him over to the "Vostok" bakery.

From the newspaper "Dvina" one day we learned about the misfortune that had befallen Alexandra Lvovna. Her husband, Doctor Vagel, had passed away. We were very sorry for her. —Too little, too little—said maman—was her chance to enjoy family life.

We were at the funeral. We met several former acquaintances there. They had already grown stooped and gray. Maman reproached them for having completely forgotten her. There was music. I walked with Andrey, and we recognized places we'd seen together the year before. —There's "chalk, screws"—we said. —And here's to you, "I. Stupel."

At the cemetery, by Karmanov's grave, recollecting, I told about how when I was visiting in Evpatoria, they'd buy Serge one roll more than me, and explain when doing so that they were paying for the extra one out of his own means. Falling behind the procession, we had a good laugh.

The Kondratyevs gave us a lift back. —The electric theater— they told us—opens one of these days. And they proposed we go see it together.

At night it was already freezing. During the day you already began coming upon places in the warm air where it suddenly got cold, like over the springs that sometimes well up in a warm river.

One day Evgenia came into my room, very mysterious. Shutting the doors behind her, she turned and put her hands up to them. Then she carefully came nearer and reported about the younger Schuster that he'd been "run in." He'd sold the sackcloth they use to cover the kneading vats in the "Vostok" bakery.

By October they'd already finished building the cathedral. On the heir to the throne's name day its "consecration" took place. I liked the image in the iconostasis of Jesus Christ drinking wine with the "beloved pupil" at his chest. I recalled Vasya. Moved, I thought about how, upon encountering me, he brings me luck, and how he helped me during my fall while descending the rope ladder into the launch.

The electric theater finally opened. At first we sat a little while in the "foyer." In the middle of it there was a pool, and in it swam little fish, rounding the aquatic plants. From the bottom rose a rock, on which were standing a little gilded boy and girl, beneath an umbrella. Water gushed from the end of the umbrella and trickled

down as if it were raining. We hadn't managed to admire it suffi-
ciently when bells already began ringing and the curtains drew back
quickly, shutting the entrances to the auditorium. —Ladies, gentlemen—I cried, seeing the rows of numbered chairs and the canvas
on the wall—it seems to be what at the exhibition was called living
photography. —Yes—confirmed maman.

23

We liked the electric cinema. It was cheap and didn't take much
time. I was there several times with maman, and went with the
Kondratyevs. We liked its "travelogues" with lakes, "dramas" in
which the wretched woman puts her baby on the rich peoples'
doorstoop, and "comics." —How silly can you get—we'd declare
from time to time, pleased. When the light flashed bright, I'd look
to see who was sitting in the chief of police's box.

The girl who showed people to their seats once seated Karl
Budrikh next to me. We hadn't greeted one another since the time I
criticized the Lutheran faith in front of him. He sat down, not looking at me. Out of the corner of my eye I saw that his face was red
from the wind and his ear was burning. His finger was almost next
to mine, and I could feel its heat. —Karl—I wanted to say.

The younger Schuster arrived from the prison castle, and his
father wouldn't let him in the house. —You've taken our family
name—he said—to jail. He was a fine figure of a man with a mustache, a machinist on the railroad, a widower, and his household
was kept by Madame Genig, whom he'd engaged when Colonel
Bobrov had died in Polotsk and she had found herself free.

Snow fell. Kondratyeva rolled up along the new road with
Andrey and admired the garrison cathedral from our window.
—But how beautiful—she said to us, glancing back. Sergey

Mitrofanov came past along the street in a little sleigh. He was driving. I remembered how sometimes I had driven Karaat. Kondratyeva's glance passed over Mitrofanov. —A tinge hefty— she said, and maman explained to her that it's a matter of feeding. Then they sat down and we listened to them for about a quarter of an hour. —The conversation of idiots—Andrey said to me when we'd left them. Again I promised myself that I'd never more, not for anything, agree to speak with him.

Sofronychev began bringing to class interesting little books, with pictures on their covers, called "Pinkerton." For a kopeck he'd let you read them, and I borrowed them, too, since I had money from the commissions for "cream."

A year earlier I could have written in my "letters to Serge" about how I liked the way the rain poured in these little books, and how Pinkerton,* after a bath, would be sitting by the fireplace, a rug on his legs, and he'd be drinking something strong. At last, he's thinking, I can rest. But suddenly a bell rings out, the housekeeper runs to open the door, letting loose a stream of imprecations as she goes.

But now I no longer wrote those letters. Like the demon* from the book "M. Lermontov," I was—alone. Bitter for me this was. —Suddenly now, I'd anticipate sometimes, wandering in the evening at dark after finishing my lessons—I'll meet somebody: Myshkin,* perhaps, or Alexey Karamazov,* and we'll get acquainted.

Once again we had a students' ball in the gymnastics hall. Madmazelle Evstigneeva sang, and Schukina performed the "sonata appassionata." Once again I was sent a note. Once again I ran away, because Stephania Grikyupel suddenly began nodding to me and started coming toward me across the circle cleared for waltzers, winking animatedly at me and making signs of some sort. By the door stood "Agatha," Gregoire's sister—colorless, with whitish hair, the nose of an Indian, and a quadrangular face. Gazing significantly, she moved her lips and shifted sideways, as if she didn't want to let me through. I was astonished—I wasn't acquainted with her.

The newspaper "Dvina" again was occupied with Alexandra Lvovna, who had won two hundred thousand in the New Year's drawing. Agitated, we hastened to congratulate her. —It's, you see, his ticket—she told us. —It wasn't for nothing I always had a premonition that something good would come of the marriage. —Yes—said maman—I remember how glad I was for you then.

We also learned that she was planning to move to the little town opposite which we had once, when I was little, spent the summer at a dacha, and where she had visited us. She had still not forgotten how she had liked the air there. —Moreover—she said—there's respectable society. —That's just—I recalled as we returned home—what I once thought: that if we won, we'd go away to live in N, where we'd be loved.

The younger Schuster got caught again, and after that it was ever back and forth: now they'd be letting him go—and then he'd walk up and down in front of the house and sometimes steal into the basement to visit Annushka—and now they'd be rearresting him. At first Madame Genig would lean out the windows and give him food, but his father didn't permit this.

Already the roads had begun to grow dark. During the day it would thaw. In the evening the sky was black, and there were especially many stars in it. More and more often I'd take out the two "women's letters" ("why are you pensive?" and "you're not like the others") and read them anew.

Churches had already begun ringing their Lenten bells. We made our confessions. Mitrofanov was in front of me, and I heard Father Nikolay, illumined by the icon lamps, mumbling to him something about "imagination and memory."

We wrote our wishes for a happy Easter to the lady from Vitebsk. In reply we received a postcard with the picture "Noli me tangere." She had already sent us this picture once. In it a striking woman kneeled before a naked Jesus Christ, who had a sheet thrown over him, and her arms reached out to him. We had a little laugh. But after reading it through maman began to cry. —Fewer and fewer—she said to me—of our friends are left. It turned out that the lady's daughter was writing to us that the lady had already died.

Just before Easter the Polish church was completed. It was white, with two quadrangular towers and a Mother of God in the recess. I liked sitting down somewhere in the evening and watching the moon disappear behind the towers and then appear again. Standing at the windows on the day of "The Body of God,"* we saw the "procession." Later the "Dvina" had a description of it, and maman said that that was "natural, because Bodrevich is a Pole."

Finally the school year was over. One hot evening maman allowed me to go to the river with Schuster. He acted amiably with me and wanted to treat me to sunflower seeds, but I wasn't accustomed to them. Near the Polish church he told me how a certain gentleman had lain prostrate, "crosslike,"* and had dropped his wallet, in which he kept a hundred rubles.

In the Nikolay Park we saw the younger Schuster. We broke into a run, but past the kitchen gardens he overtook us. Not approaching, he swore and hurled rocks at us. When he left us alone, we rested, squatting over a ditch. —Scoundrel—I said. In the distance we could see the encampments. Marches now and then reached us from over there. I recalled how once with Andrey I was standing by the river, Lieberman was sunbathing, and the orderly, like a laundress, walked with a battledore on the plank footway where they washed clothing.

Along the river's banks rafts had been heaped up. Vaulting over them we reached the river and went swimming. We jumped and pierced the sky's reflection with our feet. Then Schuster took me to the women's spot, but I saw worse than he did and all the bathers seemed to me like dim, whitish specks.

I soon began going there without him, because I felt awkward around him. He didn't read anything, and it was hard for me to think up things to talk with him about. Alone, I'd loll on the logs and listen to the water slap against them. I read Dickens's "Expectations" and it seemed to me that something extraordinary lay ahead for me as well.

One day an understamped letter arrived from Evpatoria. —What's this?—maman marveled, removing newspaper clippings from the envelope. Intrigued, she sat down to read and then said nothing. She threw the letter in the stove, and hid the clippings. I found them when she wasn't home. "A Dangerous"—was entitled the article about fifteen-year-olds that had been printed there— "Age." —So that's what it is—I said, reading through it. I noticed now that maman had begun spying on me. From that day on I tried to behave in such a way that it would be impossible for her to find out anything about me.

With Alexandra Lvovna we visited the little town where she was planning to move. It was called "Sventa-Gura." We were brought from the station by the cabby who said "bonjour." We fell into a reverie, memories beset us.

"Widow A. L. Vagel"—a plaque already stood out vividly on the gates of the one-story house made of natural stone. It had a tiled roof and an "arrow" weather vane. Formerly a "Count Michas" had lived here. We heard that he had "died in prayer."

The contractor went before us, opening doors for us. The repairs were already almost finished. In particular we liked the bathroom with windows in the cupola. You had to go down stairs into the bath.

Maman took A. L. Vagel to see Frau Anna, the widow of Doctor Ernst Rabe, and I went to take a look around Sventa-Gura. The market square was surrounded by shops. The shop signs all had pictures, under which there was the artist M. Cyperowicz's signature. The house of m-ch-t Mamonov, white, had been decorated with columns about the entrance. On a wooden balcony over the door of von Bonin's pharmacy the pharmacist's missus sat with her son. They were drinking coffee. A Polish church could be seen on the hill behind the pharmacy garden. Arranged along its cornices were statues of strenuously fussing old men and modest maidens.

I called for maman. Frau Anna affably said: —Is this your son? This is very pleasant. She treated me to pfefferkuchen.

Soon thereafter the "Philanthropic Society" turned into the "Orthodox Brotherhood." Our director became its president, and Schukina its vice-president. The brotherhood organized a concert in our gymnastics hall with Evstigneeva, Schukina, the cathedral chorus and a child phenomenon. A cross was presented to Father Fyodor from its receipts.

A. L. Vagel moved away to her new house. For almost a month we didn't hear a thing about her. Finally Frau Anna, coming with her widow's certificate to the exchequer, called on us. She told us that A. L. had visited the "palazzo," but the countess had not consented to come out to her. A. L. is planning to found an Orthodox Brotherhood in Sventa-Gura, just as we have one, and fight the Catholics. She is building a little chapel in memory of the "severance of the head" at the entrance to town, and the chapel will be painted with frescoes inside and out. —I can imagine how pretty it

will be—said maman, and it seemed to me as well that it was bound
to be beautiful.

25

When it was ready, A. L. showed it to us. She seated us in a
motorcar, and it delivered us promptly. Squattish, this little chapel
was adorned with a gilt "cupola" in the shape of a soup bowl. A. L.
taught us how to examine painting through the fist. We saw Herod,
before whom danced his fat-cheeked stepdaughter, hands propped
against her sides. I thought that thus, perhaps, had Sophie once
danced before her stepfather. John the Baptist's head lay on a table-
cloth amid loaves and cups, while his body lolled in the corner. His
neck, seen in section, was dark red with a whitish dot in the middle.
Blood spurted in an arc.

We stayed at A. L.'s until the last train. After dinner "madame"
rolled up from the city, and A. L. studied with her. —"Kee se
ressambl"—she droned on haltingly in the "study"—"s'assambl."
Then a lot of guests arrived—Sventogursk officials, pensioners,
and summerfolk. A. L. fed them and expounded on "unification"
and on "repulse."

—It's interesting—noted Repnin the postmaster—that they
have a staff for a flag at the palazzo, but they don't hang out the flag.
After that they conversed about how sad it is when you suddenly
learn that somebody is against the government, and Frau Anna,
who had kept silent, smiling pleasantly, suddenly started. —I
recall—she said—the year '05. It was terrible. People were imperti-
nent then, like wild beasts.

After that we set off for the "park." A. L. was wearing a motor-
ing hat, while in her hand she carried a whip. Striding rapidly we

walked after her along the paths. —A hymn—cried postmaster Repnin when we found ourselves on the little main square, where there was a stage. At this point everybody took off their hats. Those who had sat down stood up. Green and blue paper lanterns crackled beneath a wire stretched between the trees. An orchestra of three musicians, directed by M. Cyperowicz (artist), played. We shouted "hurrah," rejoiced, and demanded encores again and again.

—I don't understand—maman was saying as we returned, sitting in the carriage, watching the sparks outside the windows—why these fellows—Sourir and Bonin—revolve around her. I didn't say anything to her. —The "Dangerous Age"—I thought—when I'll understand this already, is fifteen, and I'm still only fourteen.

Several days after this I received a little letter. Maman wasn't home, so it didn't fall into her hands. "Please," they wrote me, "be on the boulevard."

When the time came, I left excited. I lingered in the doorway because I'd caught sight of Gorshkova. She had put on weight. Her belly had become enormous. Hardly moving, wearing a hat with flowers and a lace pelerine, she was headed for the cathedral.

After waiting for her to pass, I took off at a run. Madame Genig was standing by a tree, lying in wait for me. —I saw—she said, blocking my way—your linen being hung up over there in the courtyard. All so nice, and there's so much of it all. She tried to grab me by the arm. —If only—she sighed languidly, glancing into my eyes—Schuster's children were like you.

Because of the delay I arrived late. At the place of rendezvous I caught sight of Agatha. —Splendid—I thought. —Let her watch, and then she'll tell Nathalie all about it.

Sitting on a bench, she fidgeted and goggled her eyes. Mitrofanov walked past. I had a chat with him. He told me that he'd no longer be returning to our school but would be studying at the commercial. I realized that it couldn't be comfortable for him at our school any longer after those conversations he'd had with Father Nikolay during confession. I thought, pleased, that I'd never get caught like that. I looked around once more. Agatha leaped up and sat down again. I took off with Mitrofanov. The lady by whose invitation I had come here evidently hadn't waited for me. It was vexing.

Taking leave of Mitrofanov, I returned along the dike. Church bells were ringing. Sewage disposal men came rolling toward me, rumbling. I was astonished, recognizing among them that Osip who had once studied with me at Gorshkova's. He noticed me too, but didn't greet me. For my part, I didn't want to greet him first that evening.

At the end of summer a calamity befell Madame Strauss. The copper ham, snapping off, fell on her head, and she died before the eyes of Kapellmeister Schmidt, who had been standing with her at the entrance to the sausage shop.

The funeral was very solemn. A policeman came along and made everybody remove their caps. Then came the pastor. The first behind the hearse was Strauss. He was led by the arms by Jozes (pianos) and Jutt. Next came Madame Jutt, Madame Jozes, and Bonin's missus, who had come from the little town. Then began the crowd. In it were Pferdchen, Zachs (matches), Bodrevich, Schmidt, Grilikhess (leather), Mitrofanov's father. The bells in the Protestant church were ringing. Sad, I watched from the window. I imagined that someday, perhaps, Nathalie would be carried like that, and how, like Schmidt today, my place would be in the rear, among strangers.

26

At the prayer service Andrey stood next to me. I was pleased that

I felt no interest in him. Assuming a dignified air, I stood independently. —Two and a bird—he said to me and pointed with his head to the altar, where an image of the "trinity" hung. I didn't answer him.

As we were dispersing, I was detained in the corridor by the director. He proposed that I join the observers of the meteorological station. He explained to me that such "observers" were exempted from fees. Looking at his beard, I imagined how I'd enter and announce this news to maman, but not right away. He told me that Gvozdyov, a sixth-former, would show what needed to be done and how.

Excited, as always before making a new acquaintance, I awaited my meeting with Gvozdyov. —Would he be—I said to myself— that Myshkin for whom I'm always searching?

The next morning he ran into the classroom to see me. He was nimble and frail, with black hair and little greenish eyes. We arranged for me to go with him in the evening.

That evening resembled one in spring. The trees swayed. Tufts of loose storm clouds swiftly flew, and through them sparkled stars. A smell of forest would sometimes rush by. Gvozdyov was waiting for me on the corner. I said to him: —Hello—and the voice in which I said this pleased me: it was low, solid, not the usual.

Along the way Gvozdyov told me a little something of the teachers' lives and of the life of Ivan Moiseich and Madame Golovnyova. There was something known to him about each one. Joyful, I listened to him.

Imperceptibly we reached the school. It was dark inside. The door squealed and closed with a loud bang. Footsteps echoed. A weak light penetrated the windows from the street. The watchmen sat silently on a chest, and the ends of their home-made cigarettes shone. Gvozdyov struck "Zachs" matches. From the "physics office" we got a small lamp and a book for notes. We climbed up onto the roof toward the weather vane. The skylight was enclosed by railings. We stood a while beside them and listened to the racket on the boulevard below.

Returning, we walked past Jutt's. A lantern illumined the bas-relief by the entrance depicting an owl, and Gvozdyov informed me that this house's decorations had all been thought up by our penmanship and painting teacher Sepp. He told me that Sepp, Jutt, and the German teacher Matts came from Derpt. On holidays the three of them drank beer, sang in Estonian, and danced.

Saying good-bye, he asked me to introduce him to Gregoire. —"Gvozdyov"—I sang to the tune of "chalk, screws" when alone—"my dear Gvozdyov."

I considered what to talk about with him on future meetings, read the Raw Youth's conversations with Versilov* for an example, and looked through the "Catechism" to recall the funny places.

But the talk for which I had so prepared never took place. On the next day Gvozdyov approached me during the "break." He had a bedbug sitting on his jacket. That dampened my ardor.

I presented Gvozdyov to Sofronychev, and they became friends, and even Gregoire made a note of this in his "Calendar." He left it once on the window in the corridor, and there I came upon it. I opened it slightly. "Very"—I caught sight of an inscription—"favorite:

> BOOK—*BALAKIREV*,*
> SONG—*'ALONG THE VOLGA*,'
> HEROES—SUVOROV* AND SKOBELEV,*
> FRIEND—N. GVOZDYOV."

That autumn I didn't go to the Kondratyevs' name day. —I've been assigned a lot of lessons—I said—and moreover, I also have to run to "observation."

The weather turned cold. Maman bought me ice skates and told me to get a subscription to the skating rink. —It's good for your health—she told me. I knew that she'd found this in the article about fifteen-year-olds Karmanova had sent her in summer.

I'd take the skates and, tinkling them, go out, but I wouldn't skate, but would walk along the river toward the bend from where you could see Shavskie Drozhki in the distance, or to Griva Zemgalskaya, where the church in which A. L. had been married was.

Returning from there I'd sometimes stop by the rink. The orchestra directed by Kapellmeister Schmidt played there on a stage. Lanterns hummed and shone with a lilac light. Skaters skimmed along the fir-tree fence. Seated on the backs of benches, spectators rocked and carried on conversations in time to the music. I'd find Nathalie and watch her. Flushing, she'd be tearing across the ice with Gregoire. Gripping Gvozdyov, Agatha, squattish, would be striving vigorously and not falling behind. Karl Pferdchen, showing off, would be gliding inside a circle and performing various tricks and suddenly he'd be standing still, with one leg lifted and arms outstretched. Pale, with a fiery nose, Agatha would let her friends escape and more and more often would begin to flash past, lonely, and direct at me a significant gaze.

I noticed one girl in a blue coat there. Whenever I'd make my appearance, she'd start hanging around nearby. Once she began throwing snow at me. Not knowing what to do, I rose in embarrassment and majestically withdrew.

As always, during the Christmas holidays the students' ball took place. I went there—I hoped to receive, as always, a little letter from "Cupid's courier."

In the gymnastics hall, as in a forest, it smelled of fir trees. Between the stoves, shining, the orchestra had been arranged. Evstigneeva sang, feeble, standing at attention on stage. Everything was as always. Only Madame Strauss was missing.

Stephania stole up to me imperceptibly. —How long it's been since we've met—she said, and seizing me by the hand, began shaking it. Just in time here arrived the girl who had assaulted me once, throwing snow at me at the rink, and Stephania introduced her to me. —She's craving—she explained—to meet you. She asked me as far back as last year, but then you suddenly evaporated. The girl was nodding in confirmation of this. Robust, she had red hair, with a "Greek" nose and little narrow eyes. Her name, it turned out, was Louisa Kugenau-Petroshka.

27

—Well, I'm vanishing—said Stephania. Grimacing, she showed the palm of her hand, glanced at us sideways, like a hen, and sneaked off somewhere. Louisa remained, beaming. We walked up and down the coatroom and reported to each other what grades we had in each subject.

From the coatroom she drew me into the hall. There, with arms crossed on their chests, cavaliers and ladies were making pretzels with their legs and skipping in a circle, dancing the "Khiavata." Hopping, they would move off sideways from one another in opposite directions, and returning, would come together again. Two steps away from me Nathalie swept past with Lieberman. She was happy. Her eyes—they were brown—were raised obliquely to the left. Her hair, plaited like a grown-up's, was fluffed up, and a violet had been stuck in it.

I was handed a letter from "Cupid's courier." Written in it was: "Oho!"—and I recalled Kondratyev's notes on "Zarathustra."

Louisa studied at the "Brun Gymnasium" and brought me together with various schoolgirls from this gymnasium. For the most part they were repeaters, and not for the first time already, and girls getting on in years. Wandering in crowds, they usually spent all their time outdoors. Every evening, after joining them, I'd try to entice them to places where it would be possible that we'd meet Nathalie. I learned that she was going to Abraham's "hall for weddings and balls," where the dike turns and you can see three-quarters of the sky, and from there she would admire the comet with the Sofronychevs. I began leading my walking companions there and, stamping my feet so they wouldn't freeze, would stand there with them and make pronouncements on the comet. They saw it, but I, for some reason, never once succeeded in making it out.

We received a postcard from the Karmanovs. They proposed that I make a short visit at Shrovetide to see what sort of city Moscow was. We decided that I could go. Maman applied, and I was sent a free ticket.

I arrived in Moscow during a half-thaw. The air was misty, like in a laundry. Storm clouds hung. —The Arbat, Chulkov's house—I said, sitting down alone in a sleigh. Here and there we came upon big houses next to little hovels, and their side walls were painted with the addresses of hotels. Somewhere nearby the bells of an electric tram sounded. Multicolored churches stood here and there, cupolas glittering. Near them peasants bowed to the ground in the middle of the street, crossing themselves.

The cabby turned and we began to drag along behind some carts carrying hemp that were occupying the entire width of the lane. There I came upon Olga Kuskova. We gasped. I leaped down and she, after declaring that I'd grown up, promised to show up at the Karmanovs.

Serge had put on weight. His mouth had become fleshy, and around his lips there was already something darkening. Karmanova, wiping her pince-nez with the edge of her jacket, looked at me with interest, and I tried for that moment to put on an "air of impenetrability."

On the table I saw a photograph, covered with thick glass: next to her husband, surrounded symmetrically by three children, corpulent, with a bored face, Sophie was leaning on a balustrade upholstered in plush with little pompoms. Who would have said, I thought with melancholy, that it was she who so recently, beautiful, playing with Lieberman in a drama, had prostrated herself at his feet, and who had staggered those present, wringing her hands before him, while he, recoiling, stood unassailable, like Christ in the picture called "Noli me tangere"?

Serge showed me the little "Satyricon"* magazines. I had never seen them before. I liked them extraordinarily, and I was sorry to tear myself away from them when Serge began to drag me along to see the sights of the city.

We went out. —Were you aware, Serge—I asked when we had moved away from Chulkov's house—that your *mamachen* sent mine an essay about the dangers in being our age? Serge laughed. —In general—he said—she's an *amatrice* of the piquant. He told me that she enjoys, for example (in French, so he can't read it), a bit of the ol' Maupassant. —Is that—I asked him—an indecent book?—and he winked at me.

When we returned he showed me this book. It was called "Une vie." Its cover was wrapped in newspaper, in which there was printed that now, at last, absolutism no longer exists even in Turkey and it can now be said that all the powers of Europe are—constitutional.

In the evening Olga Kuskova was there. She recounted for us an incident from the life of a certain daredevil, and said that, it seems, the Belugins would soon be transferred to Petersburg. I and Serge saw her home, and she informed us of the easiest way to find her house: after the sign "Tea shop and cabmen's yard" you had to turn and go as far as "cabmen's yard with tea service." She whispered to me stealthily that tomorrow she'd be waiting for me at twilight.

We took our leave. Coming down the lane toward me and Serge and driving past was a grand lady drawn by black horses and a soldier on the coach-box. —Serge, remember—I said—how once you taught me a ditty about Madame Fou-Fou. We put ourselves in an agreeable mood recollecting about this and that. About that friendship which formerly had existed between us, we did not recollect.

The next day they had pancakes at the Karmanovs, and I was too lazy after eating them to go to Olga Kuskova's. On the next day after that I left. From the cab I caught sight of Ursa Major, the Great Bear. —Darling—I whispered to it: to me it somehow seemed to resemble the violet I'd once noticed in Nathalie's hair.

28

—My mama—said Louisa—would like you to give me lessons—and we arranged that tomorrow I'd drop by the "office" on the way from school, and Madame Kugenau-Petroshka would receive me out of turn. I considered what to do with the money I'd be getting from her.

Along the way sparrows hopped about and drank from puddles. On the boulevard it had melted out around each tree and you could see the turf, brown with last year's leaves. Gilded letters sparkled on signboards. By the entrance to a basement there stood a pole with a piece of cotton, and a cotton lady, wearing a black velvet hat with a feather and lit up by the sun, was sitting in a chair, rocking and, with her hands, in gloves, knitting a stocking. On the corner around which Kugenau-Petroshka lived, Agatha, returning from the gymnasium, caught up with me. She stealthily entered the passage behind me and looked to see whom I was visiting.

Kugenau-Petroshka admitted me and, having asked me to sit, seated herself, coquettish, in the dentist chair. Her face was powdered, with puffiness in places, and her hair—singed. Squinting, as Gorshkova had once done, she started bargaining with me. —Surely it's customary—she was saying—for there to be some sort of a discount for acquaintances. Disappointed, I praised myself while leaving for not having boasted before maman earlier than was proper.

The ice at the rink grew limp. It became fashionable to carry a bough of pussy willow. With a din, streams began running along the edges of the sidewalks, driven on by the street sweepers. —One sliver mounts another—cavaliers began saying, sniggering.

One hundred years, it turned out, had passed since the birth of Gogol. A speech day was organized at school. At mass Father Nikolay delivered a sermon. In it he advised us to emulate "Gogol as a son of the church." Then he served a requiem. After that we went down to the gymnastics hall. There the director, quoting "The Troyka,"* said something. The seventh-formers recited excerpts. The literature teacher declaimed an ode he'd composed himself. Afterward choristers sang it.

I was touched. I thought about the town of N, about Manilov with Chichikov, I recalled my childhood.

The "school district trustee" rolled up to our school during examinations, and I saw him in the corridor. He was lean and dark, with a scoundrelly little beard, like the rogue on the cover of a certain "Pinkerton" called "The Ill Fate of the Victoria Mines." He flunked a third of the sixth-formers. I was supposed to meet them come autumn. It could happen that I'd make friends with some of them.

Again I went to the rafts every day. There I read "Molière," which the librarian had recommended to me. And in the evening, from habit I hung around with the Brun schoolgirls. We would come across Louisa with her new boyfriend. She treated me satirically now and called me a skinflint, and was now in love with a pupil from the municipal school. This was not done among the gymnasium girls, and everyone censured her.

Sometimes, after writing an "observation," I'd linger on the school roof. I'd listen to the noises of strollers on the boulevard. I'd watch the evening glow remaining from sunset, against which the intricate chimneys of the chemist's shop showed black, and I'd think that, perhaps, at that very moment the master was drinking beer and rejoicing, enjoying the goodwill of friends.

Frau Anna, arriving one day, told us that every day now after dinner A. L. retires, alone, to the mountain and remains there until the stars' first appearance, pondering over how to draw up her will.

Maman began taking me to Sventa-Gura. In the dining room at A. L.'s I noticed a little picture that seemed very pleasant. Depicted in it was "The Last Supper." I looked to see what the artist's name was, and it turned out to be "da-Vinci." I remembered the paintings I'd seen in the gallery in Moscow, and Serge, carried away by Ioann IV, who protruded his eyes impossibly over the corpse of his murdered son.*

Both "fellows," Sourir and von Bonin, revolved as before around A. L. They would be the first to occupy the hammock by the porch and places on the sofa in the drawing room. Maman said of them that they were very poorly bred.

Once, wandering at the end of the day, I climbed the mountain and came upon A. L. She was sitting on a little hummock, huddled up, wearing a hat with a scarf, and, oldish, propping herself up with her fist, was thinking something, peering below, where you could see the palazzo. Unnoticed, I attempted from afar to hypnotize her so she'd leave her money to me.

We received a letter from Karmanova. It was rather thick, and you could easily think that there was something unwanted in it. I unglued it. In it was written that Olga Kuskova was now in

Evpatoria and Serge had begun "to live" with her, that "since he already has such a temperament, then it's better with her than with God knows whom," and that Karmanova had sometimes even been making her little gifts.

—Serge loves publicity—I said to myself and raised my eyebrows a little before the mirror.

Maman, unsealing the letter, reread it several times. Again at dinner and supper she started fixing askance on me a "piercing gaze." I was afraid that she'd suddenly make up her mind and begin saying something from "A Dangerous Age." I avoided being alone with her, and when left alone with her tried to waggle my tongue continuously so that there'd be no time for her to get a single word in edgewise.

I was with her at Utochkin.* We saw an airplane for the first time. Detaching itself from the earth, droning, it rose up and ten or so times described a large circle. Staggered, we were terribly pleased.

I returned home alone, because maman would every now and then notice acquaintances and get held up with them. Arriving after me, animated, she began criticizing to me some "candidate for a court post" whose father had died, and he had locked him in and all night, as if nothing were wrong, had had a good time in Shavskie Drozhki. Then I told her that "that's natural, since it's disgusting sitting in the same room with a corpse." Suddenly she began sobbing and screaming that now she understood what to expect from me.

For an entire month afterward, she'd glance at me, wipe her eyes, and sigh. It was silly and exasperated me.

29

I thought about Olga Kuskova, and I felt sorry for her. Clumsy, she reminded me, when I didn't see them both, of Sophie. It was still so recently that, in Shavskie Drozhki, dressed in a semi-short frock, she had been drawing for us "a girl sideways, in Little Russian dress." In the woods along the "line," when the "punitives" had gone past, she had shaken her fist after them, fervent.

The "prayer service" drew near. Together with my girlfriends I was sad that summer was ending. One day it was gray, it got dark early, drops of rain began to fall, and we dispersed, scarcely having met. Bidding me farewell, Katya Golubyova placed a chestnut in my hand. It was nice and smooth, holding it was pleasant. Raindrops dribbled quietly. In the darkness it smelled of poplar. I didn't enter the house right away, turned into the front garden and sat down on the bench. Our windows, illumined, were open. Maman was receiving Kondratyeva, and I unexpectedly heard some interesting things.

At Utochkin, where maman had worn a hat decorated with a bunch of grapes and feathers, there had been a retired colonel Pistsov, and maman had made an impression on him. He had sent her Ivanova, a retired nun—the same one Kondratyeva last year had given a blanket to quilt—and had asked how maman would regard him if he were to come to her with a proposal. —Thank— said maman—Mister Pistsov, however I have devoted myself to my son's upbringing and no longer live for myself.

I heard her begin to sniffle and say that parents sacrifice everything and see no gratitude from their children. —It's difficult to imagine—she sobbed—just how insulting their callousness is.

After that I tried not to catch the eyes of maman's acquaintants. It seemed to me that, glancing at me, they were thinking: —Callous! He's the one who insults his poor mother.

There turned out to be twelve repeaters in the class, and they all were robust fellows. As has been said, the trustee had a weakness for failing pupils possessed of an imposing appearance. They rode the high horse with us terribly, and the biggest shot of them all was Ershov. He was swarthy, with eyes that were brown, like Nathalie's. He watched superciliously, and seemed mysterious. He staggered me. I endeavored to take up with him as quickly as possible. In the school church I stood next to him, and, pointing at the icon with my head, said to him: —Two and a bird. He moved his lips and didn't look at me. I got my chestnut (Katya Golubyova's) and wanted to give it to him, but he wouldn't accept it.

I came out from roll call with Andrey. I was laughing terribly and talking very loudly, looking every now and then to see whether it was Ershov now who had passed us.

Andrey accompanied me to my house and came inside with me. As always, he opened my "Scripture" textbook. "The wilderness," he read from the chapter on "anchorite monasticism," "hitherto having been uninhabited, suddenly came to life. A great number of elders filled the above-mentioned and read in it, sang, fasted, prayed." He took a pencil and paper and drew these elders.

Karmanova, who still had some affairs remaining here, rolled up and spent several days with us. Good-humored, smiling pleasantly, she presented maman with a "Bible." —There's something wonderful here!—she said.

I overheard something when the ladies, after embracing, withdrew to maman's room, beaming. It turned out that Olga Kuskova was no longer alive. She had understood her situation poorly, and the engineer's missus had been forced to speak circumstantially with her. But she proved to be a touchy person. Setting off for the railroad embankment, she had thrown a linen sack over her head and, after getting settled on the rails, had let herself be run over by a passenger train.

The time the engineer's missus spent with us was good in that maman was distracted from me, didn't throw dramatic glances at me and accompany them with sighs.

That fall I became the tutor of a fifth-former. He was manly, bigger and heavier than I and spoke in a deep voice. Sometimes, when I was sitting with him, his father would come to us. —You, if anything's wrong—he'd say to me—let me know. I'll flog him. And he told how he flogs him in the presence of the police: at home the swine bawls and the neighbors come running. I would then remember Vasya. Childhood's poetry would revive in me.

I was busy now, and there was no time for me to walk around with the girls. In my free time I read "The Misanthrope" or "Don Juan." I had liked them during the summer, and when the pupil paid me, I bought them for myself.

That winter nothing interesting happened to me. Disillusioned, embittered, alienated, I no longer was tempted by the example of Manilov and Chichikov. I now scoffed at friendship, laughed at Gvozdyov and Sofronychev, at the pharmacy master Jutt.

On holidays, when I'd be standing in church, I'd know that ten or so steps from me, beyond the aisle, stood Nathalie. My eyesight, apparently, had gotten worse. I couldn't see her face. I only sensed which little spot was her head.

Imperceptibly we came to examination time. One morning just before the "written in mathematics" the bell in our apartment tinkled unexpectedly, and Evgenia handed me an envelope. Sealed within, written in the same hand that had written me several times through "Cupid's courier," were the problems that were to be given in the examination, and their solutions. A policeman had handed Evgenia this parcel.

30

The landowner Khaynovsky, with an enormous mustache and dressed in some kind of gray jacket with cords the likes of which I once saw on Strauss, visited us shortly after examinations to engage me for the summer for his children. I was bound by the meteorological station, and it was impossible for me to accept.

It was a pity. It seemed to me that there, perhaps, I'd see something extraordinary. I remembered one pupil last autumn telling me that he had lived at some baron's place. A cousin had come from England to visit the baroness. Wearing red trunks he had hopped into the pond from the railings of a little bridge, while the neighboring barons, who had been invited and were being served coffee, seated in the meadow—watched.

Each like the other, identical, like last summer and the one before that, without incident, the days passed. Sometimes before holidays, Gorshkova, swollen, wearing a hat with feathers, powdered, dragging the hem of her skirt along the ground, in mitts, scarcely pulling herself along, would walk past our house to the cathedral. Sometimes the younger Schuster, whistling and glancing at the windows from time to time, would saunter in front of the house. Evenings basement Annushka, returning from somewhere, would sometimes bring an acquaintance. Granny and Fedka would hop out so as not to bother them, and while they were conversing within—would stand in the street.

Once, while wandering, I found myself near the encampments, met Andrey, and we went for a stroll. As when I was little, we came upon mobile kitchens. Playbills had been pasted, and printed on them was "The Orderly—Evil-Doer." "Sunset" was trumpeted. A star appeared in the sky. —Andrey—I said—I'm reading "Serapeum."* I told him what I'd read there concerning the ancient Christians. We lamented that they were duping us in school and that we managed to learn the truth only by chance.

Putting ourselves in a critical disposition, we chattered a bit about God. We recalled how we had wanted to find out whether Serge was the "Frightful Boy."

—With Andrey—I said to myself, returning—it's nice, but somehow there's nothing poetic in him. And I remembered Ershov.

Just as the year before, A. L., ascending the mountain every day after dinner, pondered her will. Maman, in order to visit her more often, began borrowing "Ladies' World" from her. Sometimes, after reading an issue, she'd send me to cart it back.

Often, opening it on the train, I'd find something entertaining in it. For instance, we can influence a guest's emotions by the color of a lampshade. But when we want to arouse passion in a guest we should extinguish the light completely. I would have liked then for there to have been someone together with whom to have laughed at this, but there was no one.

The old ladies who visited A. L. would with pleasure initiate conversations with me. They'd ask me what I was going to be. —A doctor—A. L. would tell them for me, since I myself didn't know, and even I began to answer thus. From my chair I'd see the little picture by da Vinci, but I couldn't make anything out from that spot, and felt too self-conscious in front of everyone to get closer to it.

I would think about it every time I went past the signboards that have the laundress who's ironing, and you can see the sky in the window behind her back. I'd recall the window behind the table with the "supper" depicted in that painting.

On the day of the "transfer of the relics of Efrosinia of Polotsk" there was a "procession," and maman, putting on the hat in which Mister Pistsov had taken a fancy to her last year, went to the cathedral.

She returned from the cathedral radiant and, summoning me and Evgenia into her bedroom, began to tell us. —How beautiful it was there—she said in a pretty voice—with intonations, as if she were visiting someone—while taking off her new dress and washing herself. —There were a lot of flowers. Many ladies came specially from the dacha. And here, as if in passing, she announced to us that at the "procession" she had stood next to Missus Siou, and she had been very amiable and even, when saying good-bye, had invited maman to visit her in Shavskie Drozhki.

She rolled off there at last. It seemed to me that time didn't budge that evening. I swam for a very long time. I walked back slowly. It was sultry. Storm clouds hung. It grew dark. Noiseless lightnings flashed. In the Nikolay Park there was fidgeting in the bushes. In the streets people chuckled in the dark. Granny and Fedka were standing near the house. Madame Genig was walking from corner to corner. She detained me and told me that in such weather the fact that she is lonely makes itself felt.

For a long time I sat before the lamp over a book. Evgenia sometimes appeared in the doorway. When I wouldn't look at her, she'd noisily sigh and disappear for a while.

Maman arrived at eleven-thirty. Extremely pleased, she showed me the book she'd received for reading from Mister Siou. This book was called "So What Should We Do?" Clasping her to my heart, I stroked her, and maman told me that the Sious' maid-servant had been wonderfully trained.

—See the daughter?—I asked at last. It turned out she hadn't been at home.

From that day on maman busied herself with Evgenia's training, sewed her a headdress, and ordered her, should there happen to be free time, to knit me woolen stockings. I said I wouldn't wear them. Maman sobbed a while.

31

When we reported to school, the new director was already there.

He was red-cheeked, with purple veins, squattish, with a belly and no neck. His face was attached such that it was always somewhat lifted up and seemed to have been placed on a little lecturn.

He established a horn orchestra in our school and ordered us to wear shirts instead of jackets. In the school church he had steps made leading up to the icons. He had ordered a "rostrum" and in the gymnastics hall gave a speech from it. We learned from it, by the way, about the benefit of excursions. They, it turned out, supplement instruction in school wonderfully.

Two or three days went by, and on Saturday Ivan Moiseich appeared before us right before lessons and announced to us that in the evening we were setting off for Riga.

Not having slept enough, we arrived there in the morning and, detraining, ran off to some school to drink tea. By the station we stopped and marveled at the van drivers wearing hats and narrow liveries with capes and galloons. Their horses were harnessed without shaft bows. Trams ran past. The trees and streets had just been watered. The city was very beautiful and seemed familiar to me. It's possible it resembled that town of N I had so wanted to go to when I was little.

To begin with we visited the cathedral, then the main Protestant church. —*So sagt der apostel*—the pastor preached and gesticulated from the balcony—*Paulus!* Here Friedrich Olov approached us. He was dressed in "civvies." In his left hand he held a "bowler" and gloves.

Everyone was touched. He shook our hands, beamed, and went with us everywhere they took us. He examined with us the shoe of Anna Ioannovna in the club and the canal with swans, went to the shore, swam. —Is it possible—he admired us—you've really studied almost the entire course of sciences already? Embracing, I and he recalled how we'd conversed about Podolskaya Street, about peasants. This encounter was like some adventure from a book. I was glad.

At the shore, in the water, finding ourselves without trousers and without jackets, everyone suddenly became something other than they'd been at school. From that day I began to think about them differently.

After Riga we traveled to Polotsk. Again we didn't sleep all night, since the train departed for there at daybreak. From the windows of the carriage I saw an autumnal brown deciduous forest for the first time in my life. I recalled two lines from Pushkin.

Drowsy, we were taken to a monastery and there fed Lenten fare. Then we had to "worship the relics," and then we were told that each of us could do whatever he wanted until the train.

With the pupil Tarashkevich I found a tap near the station, and we washed our lips under it for a long time, rubbing with sand. They had swollen up, it seemed to us, from the relics, and there was some kind of disgusting taste that wouldn't come off them.

After this we walked a while and happened upon a "siding." Exhausted, we lay down between the rails. Falling asleep immediately, we awoke when it began to grow dark. We leaped up and pounded each other so as to warm up and not catch ill with rheumatism.

In the carriage I sat down next to Tarashkevich, and he told me how he'd lived at Khaynovsky's. He'd been hired for the summer when I'd had to refuse the position. He told me that Khaynovsky liked to supervise the studies, gave advice, forced his children to "lie prostrate, crosslike." Moreover, he'd come up to them from time to time and allow them to kiss his foot. I was glad I hadn't ended up there.

For our first lesson on Mondays we had "law," and it was taught to us by Nathalie's father. He was gray, wore "civvies," wore glasses, with a wart on his forehead and a small beard like Petrunkevich's. I couldn't tear myself away from looking at him. It seemed to me that in his features I discovered the features of Nathalie and of I. Stupel's madonna.

Our director loved to arrange everything ceremonially. For the "speech day" a stage had been set up in the gymnastics hall. Above it hung a picture by the penmanship and drawing teacher Sepp. Depicted in it was how Jairus's daughter* rose from the dead. Our new orchestra played. The choir sang. One after another the more comely pupils, coached by the literature teachers, climbed the stairs and declaimed, and among those let onto the stage was I.

I was applauded. Karl Pferdchen shook my hand and said: —Congratulations. The vice-president of the "brotherhood" beckoned me over to her. She informed me that she was just about to ask the director to lend me to her for a performance in the benefit concert that would be given for the brotherhood during Lent. Peysakh Leyzerakh embraced me. —You're a poet—he declared. From this time on I began to be nice to him.

When I went to take a walk in the evening, I already, it turned out, had acquired fame. The girls shook hands with me significantly. —We already know—they said. Among them I saw Louisa, who had joined us on the sly.

—I've wanted—she said to me—to converse with you unceremoniously. She praised my uncompromisingness in the bargaining with her mother that had occurred a half-year before. —It was immediately noticeable—she flattered—that you have a certain swank.

Finally the old Richter missus, the "German tutor," heard about me. She hired me for her son. He was my age, a blockhead, and I soon gave him up. Several times he said to me that it was a pity that Pushkin has been killed, and once he slipped me a sheaf of papers with verses. He had composed them himself.

I took them to school and showed some people. We laughed. Ershov unexpectedly came up and asked to have them till evening. He promised me he'd return them at "vespers."

32

I left home earlier than I needed to, and when I reached the school, turned. I told myself that I'd just start walking and meet someone.

I met a lot of people, but I didn't return with anyone, but walked on further until I caught sight of Ershov. Laughing and pulling the verses from his pocket, he nodded to me. We set off quickly. Standing in church, we glanced at one another and, concealing ourselves from Ivan Moiseich's eyes behind our neighbors' backs, not unclenching our teeth, inaudibly laughed.

Then we walked through the streets and talked about books. Ershov praised Chekhov. —That's—I said, shrugging my shoulders—the one who rakes telegraphists over the coals?

He brought "The Steppe"* to school for me, and I opened it on the spot. I was surprised. While I was reading it, it seemed to me I'd written it myself.

I took care that his interest in me wouldn't vanish. Remembering having come across something in "A Raw Youth" about some sort of indecent passage in "The Confessions," I got ahold of it. —Listen—I said to Ershov—read this.

And again I headed off early for vespers and from the school door turned and walked on until I caught sight of him.

—What a guy—he began shouting in delight, and I guessed that he was talking about Rousseau. Carried away, he gripped my arm, raised it slightly, and clasped it to himself. I quietly took it back. He wore a coat belonging to his elder brother, who had graduated from school the year before, and it was a bit small for him. It seemed to me that there was something especially sweet in this.

I gave him "The Pickwick Club,"* drew for him a lady calling her dear guests to have a bite to eat, as well as those elders who had once animated the wilderness so with their appearance.

Into the notes that I'd send him during lessons I'd introduce something or other from "Scripture" or from "literature." "The best," I'd write to him, for example, "conductor of Christian upbringing is the look. Thus, it is encumbent upon mother-educators to fasten the above-mentioned upon the educatee and express through it the three fundamental Christian feelings," or "this girl with a sensitive soul was burdened by reality and strove for the ideal." Then I'd suggest to him wandering about a bit with me in the evening.

From the viaduct we'd slowly walk as far as the "hall for weddings." It was lonely, dark, and mysterious on the dike. Sometimes drops would fall on us from the trees. The road was covered with wet leaves. We'd stand for a long time at the turning. We'd see the glow of the city lights on the storm clouds. From Griva Zemgalskaya the barking of dogs would reach us.

Ershov told me that last spring his father had quit service in excise duty and bought himself land beyond Polotsk. The whole family was living there. Ershov spoke to me poetically about the arrival at their country estate of a Polish lady, whom he and his father, carrying lanterns, had accompanied in the evening to the landing stage. I was sad that I couldn't tell him anything of that sort.

In town he lived alone at Olekhnovich's, the office worker's, and Olekhnovich praised him in the letters in which he confirmed receipt of money for the room. Also living at his place besides Ershov was the schoolmarm Edemska. Every evening at tea she'd sigh that once again she'd not time for anything and frankly didn't

know when she'd finally get to the bookstore "Oswiata"* to sub-
scribe for a half-year of the "Two Penny Newspaper."

Ershov, putting on airs and looking around, told me that his
father was a vegetarian and was even in correspondence with
Tolstoy; that when he was still an exciseman, during a trip to a certain distillery they'd palmed off on him vegetables that had been
boiled in the meat pot, and he'd eaten them not knowing, but his
soul had soon sensed that something wasn't right here, and then
he'd thrown up; and that one day on the street he'd seen an officer
beating a little soldier in the snout for failure to salute—and had
been shaking when he'd returned home and recounted this.

What amazed me a little about Ershov was his admiration for his
father, and it pleased me that, see, even Ershov was not without
weaknesses. In this he captivated me even more. I'd recall the "letters to Serge" and think that if I'd continued to compose them, then
now I'd probably have written: "Ah, Serge, sometimes a person can
be very happy."

But the allures I had had for Ershov all came to an end. Soon he
began avoiding evening meetings with me and began not answering
notes. —Are you trying to snub me?—I asked, standing, as always,
next to him at mass. Contemptuous, he said nothing to me.

That day I walked for a long time past the house in which he
lived. Snow began to fall. Olekhnovich, wearing a raincoat with a
hood and a functionary's cap, stooping, appeared on the street. He
managed to run somewhere and back during the time I was there.
His beard was straggly, narrow, and his face recalled Dostoevsky's.

With rolls wrapped in yellow paper, a little sack, edged under-
neath with a fringe, and wearing a pince-nez with a black ribbon,
the schoolmarm Edemska walked past from the corner to the gate.
Here she was already at home. Casting off her valiant bearing,
shrinking, she minced depressedly.

I felt tears at my eyes and made an effort not to let them fall. I thought about how now I'd never find out whether she'd finally subscribed to the newspaper.

At first I hoped for a long time that the matter could somehow still be reconciled. Zealously I'd sit over Tolstoy and over Chekhov, memorizing passages from them and sorting out what could be said about them if suddenly everything started up as before between me and Ershov.

In the morning of a dull day, with low storm clouds and little sprinkles in the air, we learned that Tolstoy had died. On that day I resolved to try: —Died—I said to Ershov, sitting down next to him. He looked at me, and I remembered Richter, who used to say to me that it was a pity that Pushkin has been killed.

In the evening that day maman dropped in on the Sious. She recounted with respect how at first for a long time Mister Siou wasn't at home, and then he'd arrived and brought two postcards: "Tolstoy runs away from home, with a knapsack and stick,"* and "Tolstoy comes flying to heaven and Christ embraces and kisses him."

She reported that there had been a conversation about me. The Sious were so amiable as to ask of her whether I was a lover of dancing, and she had told them no, and that this was regrettable: he who dances doesn't stuff his head with various, as the saying goes, ideas.

I turned red.

33

Since I had been saying that I wanted to be a doctor, I had at last to get to work on the Latin language. Our German teacher Matts taught it and once a week placed an advertisement in the "Dvina" to this effect. I came to an arrangement with him.

The cook would open the door for me and lead me in. —Wait a little bit—she would order. Standing on tiptoe, I'd examine the portrait of Matts, hanging on the wall over the sofa amid fans and little plaques with proverbs. Blue-eyed, with high color and a yellowish imperial and crew cut, he had been painted by our penmanship and drawing teacher Sepp.

Matts himself would appear, carrying a lamp. Setting it down, he would turn it so that the bird transfer that had been impressed onto the lampshade was properly visible to me.

—*Silva, silvae*—I'd begin to decline, looking at the transfer. Later Matts would explain something. I'd try to show that I wasn't sleeping, and to do this I'd repeat a few words after him from time to time: "*et sint candida fata tua*" or "*pulchra est.*"

Once he and I were reading "De amicitia vera."* Dreamy, he stirred his eyelids and from time to time smiled pleasantly: he was lucky in friendship.

One day, when I was returning from his place, I met Peysakh. We walked a while. Near the "hall for weddings" we stopped and, gazing at its illumined windows, listened to a waltz. I tried not to think about the fact that not so long ago I used to come here with a different companion.

Peysakh became terribly gooey. He took me by the arm, like a girl, and promised to give me a copy of that ode our literature teacher had composed the year before. I remembered only its ending:

Russians, our poet's dear sept,
Brethren of he who for thee wept,
Attend me, and let us now send
An urn unseen of tender
Feeling's tears
In concert to heights unbound,
To the empyreal laird,
With words of petition by good men shared:
Glory eternal to Gogol.

—Let's stop in—he suggested when, repeating these few lines, we entered the lane in which he lived. I went with him, and he gave me the ode. We laughed at it for a long time. I could have gotten it earlier, and then it could have been Ershov laughing with me.

Christmas was drawing near. The high school students were coming home. Skipping out at the "big recess," we'd see them. In a year, we anticipated, we too would be wearing that uniform, would show up at the school, and, standing in a crowd, facing the director's windows, would smoke cigarettes with an air of independence.

Gvozdyov came. He was studying now at the Vladimir Military School. He unexpectedly had grown, become broader than he was. It wasn't easy recognizing him. Manly, stomping along the sidewalks with the soles of his shoes, he would bring the tips of his gloved fingers to the peak of his cap and jerk up his nose, delighting the girls. He didn't drop in to see Gregoire, and upon encountering him treated him slightingly.

On the day they dismissed us I saw the schoolmarm Edemska driving to the train. She was sitting up straight, solemn. A basket with her things stood on the sleigh seat beside her. It could well have been that just now she'd been helped carrying this basket to the gate by Ershov.

On the first day of Christmas the mailman brought letters. Evgenia, wearing a white headdress, absurd, like a cow wearing a saddle, brought them in: Karmanova, Vagel A. L., Frau Anna, and some other people sent holiday greetings—to maman. Me no one wrote. And there was nowhere I could expect a letter from. Outside the window snow fell heavily. Just so, perhaps, was it also falling that morning over the "land" beyond Polotsk.

Blyuma Katz-Kagan was thickset, squattish, and her face resembled that of the red-cheeked troyka driver displayed in the window of the "Paradise for Children" shop. She had graduated last year from the "Brun Gymnasium" and had departed for Kiev for courses in dentistry. Coming outside one warm evening, when the drainpipes were dripping, I saw her near the house. She had come for the holidays.

—Have you read—she said to me—Chukovsky:* "Nat Pinkerton and Contemporary Literature"? This title excited my curiosity. I had read Pinkerton, but as to "contemporary literature," I thought that was—something like "The Red Laugh." I imagined vividly how they must laugh at that in this book. I wanted very much to read it.

From the dike I looked at Janek's house. In the Sious' windows someone was moving. Perhaps it was Nathalie. A waltz could be heard from the skating rink. I said that the ice was soft today, and Blyuma agreed with me.

—But that's not the point—she declared. —I recently was reading a certain interesting novel. And she recounted it.

A gentleman was traveling with a lady.* They liked Italy most of all. They weren't husband and wife, but behaved as if they were married.

—Well, what do you think of them?—she wanted to know. I was amazed. —Not a thing—I said.

Opposite the "hall for weddings," when we were standing in the dark and could hear the noise of the electric station, the orchestra in the distance and the barking of dogs, near and far away, Katz-Kagan went limp. Clasping my arm, she was silent and collapsed against my side. I was forced to move away from her. I asked her if she remembered how people once came here to look at the comet. She told me that we ought to meet again, and informed me of how to write to her poste restante: "K-K-B, 200 000."

Over the course of that winter Tarashkevich invited me several times, and I went to see him. Besides me there were Gregoire and one of the "A" students. He would show us how problems of various kinds were solved. Then we were fed and treated to fruit liqueur. Goodwill sprung up between us. Saying good-bye, we'd stand in the hallway for a long time, looking at one another, laugh, and again and again begin to shake hands but simply couldn't break up.

During these minutes I regarded with particular tenderness Sofronychev. —You meet—I'd think, gazing upon him affectionately—every day with Nathalie. Just like me, you know from experience what the perfidy of friends is.

Tarashkevich shared a bench at school with Schuster. He blabbed to us that Schuster visits Podolskaya Street. —Schuster— I said to myself, staggered. I remembered how once I hadn't found in him anything interesting. —How little, after all, we know of people—I thought—and how incorrectly we judge them.

Leaving early in the morning, I began waiting for him. —Schuster—I said and took him by the arm. Straightaway I asked him whether it were true. Flattered, he told me everything. He goes on Fridays, since that's the day they have the examination there. He demands the books and finds out who's healthy. The rooms there are not partitioned to the very top. One day his younger brother turned out to be there next door. He climbed over the wall and began fighting, using a chair. Now they don't admit him into the houses: If he wants to go there, then let him behave as befits one.

34

Father Nikolay, covering my head with a black apron, was curious this year whether I had "committed adultery." I asked him to explain to me how this was done, and, not persisting, he let me go. I ran off, congratulating myself that the last confession of my life was over.

Once again I had to perform onstage—on the day that "emancipation of the peasants" was celebrated. I read the verses very poorly, so that the vice-president of the brotherhood would be disillusioned, and so that Ershov wouldn't think I was a complete idiot.

Peysakh praised me greatly. —You showed them once—he said—that you can do it, and that'll do for them. He now approved of everything I did. But it wasn't his approval I wanted.

Already it felt as though spring would soon be here. In "Paradise for Children" balls already were being displayed in the windows in place of sleds. Peoples' faces were already becoming brown. I gave up Latin.

—All the same, I won't manage to get through the whole course—I would say, and, besides, it had now become clear to me that I didn't want to be a doctor.

I managed to find out from the Latin lessons, incidentally, that "Noli me tangere," the inscription under the little picture with Christ wrapped in a sheet and a maiden at his feet, meant "Don't touch me."

Once again examinations were upon us. Once again we dreaded that the "school district trustee" might show up. We were glad when we suddenly learned that someone had killed him with a rock.

There was a requiem. Father Nikolay gave the sermon. Soon thereafter they printed in the newspaper a report from the doctor by whom the trustee had usually been treated. It was turning out that the deceased was a degenerate and a maniac. He would fail the pupils with attractive appearances for the sake of some sort of particular feelings. While he was alive, this was supposed to be concealed, since it was forbidden to violate a "medical confidence."

They went on strike at Grilikhess's. Maman was boiling, and I was amazed at her. —If only I knew how—she'd say to me—then I'd go and work for him myself these few days.

Once during examinations Tarashkevich came running for me. Already awaiting us at his house were Gregoire, full of mystery, and the amiable A-student. Extracting an envelope, Gregoire laid before us a piece of paper with problems. —Now then—he said. The A-student solved these problems for us. The next day they were given to us on the examination.

We crammed to the point of exhaustion. We were sleeping three or four hours a day, and maman was eating her heart out. —When—she'd say—will this end? Getting ready for bed, she'd bring me a handful of fruit drops for the night.

At last came the day when it was all over. We received "certificates." From the "rostrum," on which a glass of lilies of the valley was standing, parting words were spoken. Now falling asleep, now starting and opening my eyes for a minute, I saw how after the director the literature teacher came to be up there. He stuck out his lip, looked at his mustache, and tugged it. —Truth, good—he eloquently exclaimed, as usual—and beauty!

Evening arrived, and in the little "observations" book I made my final note. Beneath the weather vane on the roof I lingered, as always. I thought about how I'd often stood here.

Kanatchikov, receiving the apartment money, congratulated me. He didn't leave at once, told us that his son had gone mad because he hadn't passed the entrance examination for the technological institute. —He passed all the sciences—Kanatchikov told us—and didn't pass only the plinth that glues rooms together.

Everybody entered one institute or another. I still hadn't thought of anything for myself. I asked if there weren't some little place where they'd admit you not by means of examinations and not having chased after grades in mathematics, and it turned out there was. I bought a linen envelope and sent my documents in it. I was soon sent a letter saying that I was admitted.

In the "police station," where I went for a "certificate of political loyalty," I saw Vasya. He walked quickly past. —No, madame—he was saying without halting to a petitioner running relentlessly after him. From habit, pleasantly disturbed, I followed him with my eyes, and when he vanished, I thought that, perhaps, he was at this very minute starting to flog someone who'd been brought to the police for that purpose.

Schuster was staying with his father's sister in a "pastorate" on the other side of the Dvina, and I didn't encounter him. Peysakh sometimes dropped in to see me. I compiled for him a list of the days on which maman went off to be on duty. Once he showed me the ode that our former literature teacher had composed for this year's celebration of the "emancipation of the peasants." I read through it without interest. The school no longer mattered to me.

Peysakh was supposed to leave with his family for America at the end of summer. He already had accustomed himself to a "bowler" hat and instead of his former glasses wore a pince-nez with a ribbon. Once, when walking with him and falling a half-step behind, my glance happened to fall through its glass.

—Wait up—I said, dumbstruck. I took the pince-nez off his nose and brought it toward mine. That very day I visited an eye doctor and put lenses on my nose.

I now saw faces on the street distinctly, read numbers on cabbies' droshkies and signs across the road. On a tree I now saw all the little leaves. I looked in the window of the "Faience" shop and saw what was on the shelves inside. I saw twelve plates, set in a row, on which Jews wearing rags had been painted, with the inscription "They gave credit."

On the other side of the river, astonished, I saw people, a herd, Griva-Zemgalskaya's mill. Whistling, down to the shore came the Osip with whom I'd studied together while getting ready for the preparatory-class examination.

Quickly throwing everything off, brown, he was left wearing only a little round hat and ran off in it toward the water. Running past, he glanced at me out of the corner of his eye. I felt like saying "Hello" to him, but I didn't dare.

I approached the house where Ershov had lived last winter. I saw a design made of nails on the gate that he'd opened so many times. It screeched. Across its threshold, stooping, stepped Olekhnovich. He was wearing that same raincoat with the hood I'd seen him wearing in winter. I now saw that the raincoat's fastening consisted of two lions' heads and a chain linking them.

In the evening, when it got dark, I saw that the stars are very many, and that they have beams. I began to think about the fact that until then everything I'd seen I'd seen incorrectly. I'd have been interested in seeing Nathalie now and finding out what she looked like. But Nathalie was far away. She was spending summer this year in Odessa.

```
        »)»)» ««(«
```

Notes

2   To Alexander Pavlovich Drozdov: Dobychin dedicates his
     novel to a young man, a simple worker and former *besprizornik*
     (one of the millions of homeless, familyless children who
     roamed the Russian countryside in the years after the
     Revolution and Civil War), who lived in his communal apart-
     ment on the Moika Canal in St. Petersburg.

3   Chichikov: The rogue-protagonist of Nikolai Gogol's
     picaresque *Dead Souls* (1842), in which he pursues an elaborate
     fraud by "buying" lists of deceased serfs ("souls") whose names
     have not yet been removed from the census rolls. The town of
     N is the provincial Russian setting for this comic-satiric novel,
     and its inhabitants, cartoonish monomaniacs, prove that the
     "Dead Souls" of the title refers not only to the deceased.

3   *proskomidia:* The first part of the Eastern Orthodox liturgy.

4   Madmazelle: This is an exact rendering of the spelling in the
     Russian text, which reflects the child narrator's imperfect com-
     prehension. While there are antecedents for transliterating the
     French form of address as it is generally pronounced (usually
     "mamzel'"), the standard literary rendering of "mademoiselle"
     in Russian is either the phonetically accurate "mademuazel" or
     the immediate use of the Latin lettered word.

6   Manilov: A mawkish, ingratiating landowner in *Dead Souls,*
     whom Chichikov "befriends" in order to acquire his dead
     souls.

6   *skrynka:* A small chest. It is both a Lithuanian and an antiquat-
     ed Russian word.

6   Pyotr m-ch-t Mitrofanov: This rendering reflects the child's
     too literal reading of a merchant's shop sign; in the Russian
     original, "Pyotr k-ts Mitrofanov," an abbreviation of "Pyotr
     kupets Mitrofanov" (Pyotr the merchant Mitrofanov).

6   Polish priest: The Russian word here, *ksendz,* refers to a Roman
     Catholic priest in Poland or a Polish Roman Catholic priest in
     Eastern Europe. Religion and nationality, and bigotry attached
     to both, are closely linked in the novel. Thus, three types of
     church (and five different varieties of Christianity) appear
     here—Roman Catholic (with a Polish or Latvian and
     Lithuanian congregation and priest), Eastern Orthodox (with a
     Russian congregation and priest), and Protestant (with a largely
     German or Latvian congregation and pastor; historically, Latvia
     was predominantly Lutheran)—each identified by a single
     Russian word, for which there exists no direct equivalent in
     English: Polish (Roman Catholic) church = *kostyol;* Russian
     (Eastern) Orthodox church = *tserkov';* Protestant church =
     kirka. ("Uniates," Jews, and Russian Orthodox "Old Believers"
     are also represented.) These separate words also reflect the fact
     that for the child, as for the adults whose biases he generally
     reproduces as fact, these three institutions and their spiritual
     leaders are three distinct entities, not variants on the same
     essence. For adults, these three separate institutions embody
     national, historical, political, and social significance, often of a
     prejudiced nature, that goes far beyond spiritual matters.
     Likewise, there are different words for Roman Catholic (*ksendz*)

and Russian Orthodox (*sviashchennik*) priests, and for Protestant pastors (*pastor*).

7   *kissel:* A sweet dish of Russian origin, made from fruit juice mixed with sugar and water, which is boiled and thickened with potato or corn flour.

8   Leykin, Nikolai Aleksandrovich (1841–1906), Russian humorist and journalist, who described in stories, plays, sketches, and novels the manners and morals of the Petersburg merchant and bureaucratic classes. Leykin published more than two hundred of Chekhov's early comic sketches in his humor magazine *Splinters (Oskolki)*.

8   an offering of bread and salt: Traditional Russian symbol of hospitality, offered to guests.

8   Uniates: Today known as the Eastern Rite or Eastern Catholic Church, these are any of the several Eastern Christian Churches that originated as Eastern national or ethnic Christian institutions but later established union (thus "Uniates") with the Roman Catholic Church. In this union they accept the Roman Catholic faith and recognize the Roman pope as head of the church, but retain their own unique characteristics in matters such as liturgy, sacred art, and institutional structure.

9   Themistoclius and Alcides: Manilov's young sons in *Dead Souls*.

11 *akathistus:* A church service comprising religious song, performed standing.

12 the blessing of the waters: On January 6 in the Russian Orthodox calendar the baptism of Christ is celebrated by a priest submerging the cross in a body of water (often through a hole in the ice). The water thereby acquires wonder-working

powers and is distributed to churches for baptisms and other ceremonial blessings. Frequently this ceremony is followed by worshippers themselves plunging, or dipping their babies, into the icy water.

15 Selifan: Chichikov's coachman in *Dead Souls*.

17 *tey trrinken:* German for "to drink tea" is *tee trinken*. The present rendering notes the mocking children's imperfect imitation of the local Germans.

18 *Ei, zwei, drei* (Yiddish): "One, two, three"; the *ei* is a Baltic region variant of the Yiddish word for "one."

18 "The Beloved Pupil": "Liubimyi uchenik" conventionally would be translated as "The Favorite Disciple" or "The Beloved Disciple." The "beloved disciple" or "the disciple whom Jesus loved" plays an important role in the Gospel According to John. While his precise identity is not ascertainable from the biblical text, this disciple is traditionally regarded to be John the Apostle himself (also known as John the Evangelist and Saint John the Divine), who, likewise, is not named in the Fourth Gospel. The "beloved disciple" is he to whom Christ, while on the cross, entrusted the care of his mother. The word *uchenik* (disciple), however, also means "pupil" or "schoolboy" in modern standard Russian. Given the Dobychin child's identification of Vasya Strizhkin—his own, personal "beloved pupil"—with Jesus' beloved disciple/pupil, "John by the cross," it is clear that the child makes no distinction between these slightly different senses of *uchenik*. To maintain this associative linkage I have chosen to stray from the most "literal" translation to one more essential.

18 *Pan Khristus z martvekh vsta:* In Polish in the original (but in Cyrillic letters, transliterated here): Christ is risen from the dead.

22 *baranki:* Dry ring-shaped rolls.

26 Madonna of Saint Sixtus (*Madonna sviatogo Siksta*): Raphael's Madonna di San Sisto, popularly known as the "Sistine Madonna" (*Siktinskaia Madonna*), a painting which played a considerable role in nineteenth-century Russian society and culture. James Billington (*The Icon and the Axe* [New York: Knopf, 1967], 348–50) explains that "the Sistine Madonna" became a "kind of icon of Russian romanticism," the "highest symbol of the classical culture that the Russians longed to share and the quintessence of ideal beauty to their romantic imagination." Dostoevsky kept a print of it over his writing desk as "the personal icon of his own effort to reconcile faith and creative power," "a symbol of the combination of faith and beauty which he hoped would save the world." Zhukovsky sang its praises in verse, Herzen in prose. Belinsky condemned it, while Pisarev and Bakunin used it in notorious political slogans as a symbol of useless beauty and misplaced adoration. A. A. Ivanov, whose portrayal of the "Noli me tangere" theme plays an important role in the *The Town of N*, kept his own sketch of the Sistine Madonna before him while working on his monumental "Appearance of Christ to the People."

27 color of Navarino flame and smoke: In *Dead Souls*, the color of Chichikov's suit.

27 Admiralty: One of St. Petersburg's most prominent buildings, the nucleus of Peter the Great's original city, located on the left bank of the Neva at the western terminal of Nevsky Prospekt. The spire of its main gate is topped with a weather vane in the form of a ship, a celebrated city landmark.

29 Tusenka: A diminutive form of the Russian name Natalya (Natasha).

30 a certain picture with the inscription "All in the Past":

Presumably the well-known painting of that name by Vasilii Maksimov (1889), which hangs in Moscow's Tretyakov Gallery.

31 *prosze* (Polish): Please, if you please.

33 Miracle at the Borki Trainwreck: The railroad disaster of October 18, 1888, near the town of Borki, which, by a miracle, Tsar Alexander III and his family survived. Their train derailed, killing twenty-three people and seriously wounding dozens more. The imperial dining car, in which the tsar, his wife, and several of their children were then seated, was completely destroyed, but the royal family emerged with only minor injuries.

35 Yat (Yat'): The comical name of a comical figure, a telegraphist, in Anton Chekhov's farcical one-act play *The Wedding* (*Svad'ba*). It is also the name of an old Russian letter replaced by *e* in 1918. Again Dobychin's children remain comically poor readers, misreading farce as drama, failing to detect irony, and confusing fiction with real life.

36 Mowgli: A child who lives among wild beasts in Rudyard Kipling's classic story collections *The Jungle Books* (1894 and 1895), which have enjoyed unsurpassed popularity with Russian children since their publication.

37 Fright Night (*Strashnaia noch'*): A more informed understanding of this term might be "Judgment Night," by analogy with "The Last Judgment" or "Doomsday" (*Strashnyi sud*), for it refers to the Jewish religious New Year, Rosh Hashanah, which initiates a ten-day period of self-examination and penitence, and thus is often known as the Day of Judgment. Each Jew reviews his relationship with God, the Supreme Judge. Dobychin's child, given to misreadings of other cultures' rites

and iconography, most likely hears in the word *strashnyi* the more common usage "frightful," "dreadful," "terrible," or "horrible," connecting it in his imagination with other local anti-Semitic lore, including the idea of little Christian boys disappearing and the making of "pigs' ears." This "frightful" also recalls the "Frightful Boy," the *strashnyi mal'chik* of chapter 2.

37 pig's ear: To make fun of Jews; to clench together material of a jacket into the shape of a pig's ear (pork being forbidden).

38 lint: See Leo Tolstoy's *War and Peace,* part 5, chapter 26, where, during the Napoleonic wars, an army doctor says to Nikolai Rostov, "Just think, I have three hospitals to look after alone—more than four hundred patients. It's a good thing the Prussian charitable ladies send us coffee and lint—two pounds a month—or we would be lost.'"

39 "Noli me tangere" (Latin, "Don't touch me"): This refers to the scene in John 20:17 where Christ admonishes Mary Magdalene not to touch (or hold) him as he emerges, resurrected, from the tomb. "Noli me tangere" is an important figure within Christian iconography, both in the Eastern and Western traditions. In the latter, it is the subject of innumerable paintings, including important works by Duccio, Giotto, Fra Angelico, Corregio, Titian, Veronese, Dürer, Rembrandt, and A. A. Ivanov. The child's later (chapter 24) description of the same postcard ("In it a striking woman kneeled before a naked Jesus Christ, who had a sheet thrown over him, and her arms reached out to him") corresponds closely, and most likely refers to Ivanov's rendition, which was painted in 1834–36 and hangs in the State Russian Museum in St. Petersburg (although that work is formally entitled *The Appearance of Christ to Mary Magdalene after Resurrection*). Sent by the young artist from Italy, this work made an extremely favorable

impression and won Ivanov the title of "academic." In his interpretation of "Noli me tangere," Ivanov depicts a Jesus who is clearly rejecting the supplication or touch of the Magdalene. The similarity here to the child's romantic prototype of Sophie on her knees, supplicating a resolute and implacable Alexander Lieberman ("Oh, Alexander, forgive me"), and his subsequent, imagined scenes in which a repentant Natalya Pushkin begs forgiveness of her own implacable Alexander (Pushkin), and a love-struck Natalya Siou supplicates the child himself, is, of course, striking, as the child himself eventually recognizes.

40 Pleve, Vyacheslav Konstantinovich (1846–1904): Deeply conservative Russian imperial statesman, minister of interior from 1902. An upholder of autocracy, the police-bureaucratic state, and class privilege. Pursued Russification policies against minority national groups, encouraged anti-Semitic propaganda, suppressed liberal local government (*zemstvo*) activity and all revolutionary movements. Supported policies that led to the Russo-Japanese War. Assassinated by a Socialist Revolutionary Party member.

42 cross yourself with two fingers: Russian religious dissenters, known as Old Believers, who refused to accept the liturgical reforms imposed on the Russian Orthodox Church by the Moscow patriarch Nikon in 1652–58, to this day make the sign of the cross with two fingers, not the three fingers used by those in the reformed church.

43 *kauliang* (Russian = *gaolian*): sorghum (from which porridge, pancakes, and alcohol are made); *fan-jiao* (Russian = *fanza*): peasant house.

45 Gogol in Vasilevka: The estate of Nikolai Gogol's parents, where the writer spent his childhood.

45 Letts: Latvians. Historically, landowners in Latvia had been of German (and noble) descent. The indigenous Letts were predominantly landless peasants. St. John's—or Midsummer's—Eve is traditionally an important Latvian national festival.

45 Stessel, Anatolii Mikhailovich (1848–1915): Russian general. At the outbreak of the Russo-Japanese War (1904) he was placed in command at Port Arthur. After a prolonged defense he surrendered the city to the Japanese. He was at first lionized by the press and honored by the tsar as a war hero. Later, however, when it became known that he had surrendered against the counsel of his senior officers and despite the fact that he still had an adequate supply of men and materials, he was vilified and brought to court martial. In 1908 he was sentenced to death, a sentence that was later commuted to ten years incarceration. The tsar granted him a pardon in 1909.

46 Witte, Sergei Yulyevich (1849–1915): Russian minister of finance (1892–1903) who, despite detesting constitutionalism, served as the Russian Empire's first constitutional prime minister (1905–6). Sought to combine authoritarian rule with economic modernization along Western lines. Conducted peace negotiations with Japan in 1905 and obtained unexpectedly favorable terms for Russia. Nevertheless remained an unpopular figure.

48 Black Hundreds (*chernosotentsy*): Reactionary, anti-Semitic groups formed in Russia during and after the 1905 revolution to support Orthodoxy, autocracy, and Russian nationalism, and to conduct raids on revolutionary groups and pogroms against Jews.

49 *The Red Laugh:* A novella (1905) by Leonid Nikolaevich Andreev (1871-1919) in the form of a diary written by a madman. A passionately antimilitarist work, written in response to

the horrors of contemporary warfare in the Russo-Japanese conflict.

51 Petrunkevich, Ivan Ilyich (1843–1928): Liberal Russian political activist. Founder and chairman of the illegal "Union of Emancipation," which stood for a constitutional monarchy, universal suffrage, partial transfer of land holdings from estate owners to peasants, and an eight-hour workday; editor of the newspaper *Rech'* (*Speech*); one of the founding members of the Constitutional-Democratic (Kadet) Party and deputy of the First State Duma.

51 Muromtsev, Sergei Andreevich (1850–1910): Russian jurist, publicist, and political figure. One of the founders of the Constitutional-Democratic (Kadet) Party, and from 1905 a member of its Central Committee. In 1906 Muromtsev became president of the first Russian State Duma.

55 lottery allegri: A sort of raffle, popular at pre-Revolutionary Russian social events, in which lots are drawn immediately after a chance has been bought (usually in the form of an admission ticket).

57 State Duma: State Assembly. The elected legislative body that was created after the 1905 revolution and which, together with the State Council, made up the imperial Russian legislature from 1906 until the February Revolution of 1917.

57 The panorama depicts the siege of Sevastopol (1854–55) by Allied forces during the Crimean War.

59 *Quo Vadis?*: Extremely popular historical novel (1896), concerning Christianity in the time of Nero, by Polish Nobel laureate Henryk Sienkiewicz (1846–1916).

59 *The Life of Jesus:* By David Friedrich Strauss (1808–77), German theologian and biographer. His *Leben Jesu* (1835) cre-

ated an immense sensation by denying the historical credibility of the Gospel narratives of Jesus' life. While accepting the basic fact of an historical Jesus, Strauss, interpreting Christianity through Hegelian historical concepts, understood the Gospels' supernatural occurrences as myths that developed, along lines anticipated by Old Testament prophecy, after Jesus' death.

64　Pinkerton: Nat Pinkerton, hero of popular detective novels that enjoyed particular vogue in turn-of-the-century Russia and colored the imaginations of Russian writers (notably Valentin Kataev) whose childhoods coincided with their popularity. The name Pinkerton derives from the real-life American investigator Allan Pinkerton, who founded the famous detective agency. One of the first to examine this phenomenon from a scholarly perspective was the young Kornei Chukovsky (see note below).

64　demon: The protagonist of Mikhail Lermontov's romantic long poem of the same name.

64　Myshkin: Prince Myshkin, the gentle, Christlike, but ultimately all-too-human protagonist of Fyodor Dostoevsky's novel *The Idiot* (1868–69).

64　Alexey Karamazov: "Alyosha" is the youngest of Fyodor Dostoevsky's three Karamazov brothers of the novel of that name. He is the brother who is identified with Christian ideals, and who "loves life more than its meaning."

66　"The Body of God": In the Russian text this is given in Polish—"*božego cialo*"—but in Cyrillic transcription (*bozhego tialo*). The child is likely to understand this literally as "The Body of God." In fact, it is the Roman Catholic feast of Corpus Christi, or "The Body of Christ," which celebrates the Real Presence of the body (corpus) in the Eucharist. This feast began in the thirteenth century, and in the fifteenth century became, in effect, the Western church's principal feast. The feast's most prominent feature is the procession (which was traditionally followed by miracle plays). There is no comparable feast in the Eastern Orthodox Church. The feast's name and iconography are likely to exert on unenlightened imaginations the same powerful sense of bizarre mystery as the Jewish "Fright Night."

66 had lain prostrate, "crosslike" (*"Lezhat' kshizhom"* [*krzyzom*]): In the Russian text this is a fixed expression, repeated in a local patois which variously combines with a predominant Russian component elements of Polish, Lithuanian, Latvian, and even German and Yiddish. It means "to be lying prostrate, with arms flung out, like a cross," and may be regarded as one of the novel's many fraudulent Christ symbols.

73 the Raw Youth's conversations with Versilov: Dostoevsky's protagonists in the novel *Podrostok* (1875), variously translated into English as *A Raw Youth*, *The Adolescent*, and, most recently, *An Accidental Family*.

73 Balakirev, I. A. (1699–?): Court jester during the reigns of Peter the Great, Catherine I, and Anna Ivanovna. In 1830 K. A. Polevoi published the *Collected Jokes of Balakirev*, in reality an anthology of humorous anecdotes from world culture, upon which Balakirev's legendary fame as a witty fool has grown. Numerous such anthologies of anecdotes supposedly by or about Balakirev have been published in Russia since.

73 Suvorov, Aleksandr Vasilevich (1729–1800): One of Russia's greatest military heroes, who attained the unprecedented rank of generalissimo and never lost a battle. Suvorov's fame derives from his achievements in the Russo-Turkish War of 1787–91, in the French Revolutionary Wars, in suppressing the Russian peasant revolt led by Emelyan Pugachov (1774), in crushing

the nationalist-revolutionary movement in Poland in 1794, and for his dramatic escape from a French encirclement in Switzerland in the winter of 1799–80. He was also the author of a celebrated military treatise.

73 Skobelev, M. D. (1843–82): Russian infantry general who played prominent roles in Russia's conquest of Turkistan and in the Russo-Turkish War of 1877–78. Known as the "White General" for the white uniform and white horse he took to battle.

77 *Satyricon (Satirikon)*: Liberally oriented comic-satirical weekly magazine, published in St. Petersburg between 1908 and 1914. Among its founding contributors were Sasha Chernyi and Nadezhda Teffi.

79 "The Troyka": The famous panegyric that concludes volume 2, book 1 of Gogol's *Dead Souls,* in which the narrator compares Russia to a speeding troyka and wonders whither she flies.

80 carried away by Ioann IV, who protruded his eyes impossibly over the corpse of his murdered son: Ilya Repin's famous painting of Ivan the Terrible, looking horrified as he holds the son he has just murdered. In the Tretyakov Gallery, Moscow.

81 Utochkin, Sergey Isayevich (1876–1916): One of the first Russian airplane pilots, popularizer of aviation, aerial balloonist, boxer, fencer, wrestler, bicycle racer, racecar driver, showman. Figures prominently in boyhood memories of writers of Dobychin's generation. See, for example, Yury Olesha's *No Day without a Line* and "The Chain," and Valentin Kataev's *A Shattered Life* (published in English translation with the title *A Mosaic of Life*).

85 Serapeum: The name of ancient Egyptian temples dedicated to

the cult of the Greco–Egyptian god Serapis (Sarapis). The Serapeum at Alexandria, which housed the renowned Ptolemain library, and which was the Ptolemaic cult's sanctum, was destroyed in A.D. 391 by Patriarch Theophilus in his brutal campaign against Roman paganism.

90 Jairus's daughter: The Gospel According to Mark 5:21–42 tells of Jesus resurrecting from the dead the daughter of Jairus (Iair), one of the leaders of the synagogue.

91 "The Steppe": A classic of Russian "childhood" fiction, Anton Chekhov's long story (1888) describes a journey across the Ukrainian steppe through the eyes of a young boy, who experiences a full slice of life: boredom, cruelty, ignorance, deceit, kindness, and beauty.

92 *The Pickwick Club:* Charles Dickens's *The Posthumous Papers of the Pickwick Club* (1837), known familiarly in English as *The Pickwick Papers*, is known in Russian as *The Pickwick Club* (*Pikvikskii klub*).

93 the bookstore "Oswiata": In Polish in the original, in Cyrillic transcription (*do ksendzharni "Osviata"*). Oswiata means "enlightenment" or "education."

94 "Tolstoy runs away from home, with a knapsack and stick": The great writer Leo Tolstoy did in fact "run away from home" at the age of eighty-two after a breach with his family. He contracted pneumonia several days later and died of heart failure in the stationmaster's house at the village of Astapovo, November 20, 1910.

95 "De amacitia vera" (Latin): "On True Friendship," from *Laelius, On Friendship* (Laelius de Amicitia) (44 B.C.), in which Roman writer, statesman, and philosopher Marcus Tullius Cicero Laelius (Cicero) engages in a dialogue on friendship with the young Scipio.

96 Chukovsky, Kornei Ivanovich: Pseudonym of Nikolai Vasilyeiich Korneichukov (1882–1969), Russian literary critic, translator, language theoretician, author of classic children's books.

97 A gentleman was traveling with a lady: Blyuma recounts the basic plot of Tolstoy's *Anna Karenina*.

European Classics

Jerzy Andrzejewski
Ashes and Diamonds

Honoré de Balzac
The Bureaucrats

Heinrich Böll
Absent without Leave
And Never Said a Word
And Where Were You, Adam?
The Bread of Those Early Years
End of a Mission
Irish Journal
Missing Persons and Other Essays
The Safety Net
A Soldier's Legacy
The Stories of Heinrich Böll
Tomorrow and Yesterday
The Train Was on Time
What's to Become of the Boy?
Women in a River Landscape

Madeleine Bourdouxhe
La Femme de Gilles

Karel Capek
Nine Fairy Tales
War with the Newts

Lydia Chukovskaya
Sofia Petrovna

Grazia Deledda
After the Divorce
Elias Portolu

Leonid Dobychin
The Town of N

Yury Dombrovsky
The Keeper of Antiquities

Aleksandr Druzhinin
Polinka Saks • The Story of Aleksei Dmitrich

Venedikt Erofeev
Moscow to the End of the Line

Konstantin Fedin
Cities and Years

Fyodor Vasilievich Gladkov
Cement

I. Grekova
The Ship of Widows

Vasily Grossman
Forever Flowing

Stefan Heym
The King David Report

Marek Hlasko
The Eighth Day of the Week

Bohumil Hrabal
Closely Watched Trains

Ilf and Petrov
The Twelve Chairs

Vsevolod Ivanov
Fertility and Other Stories

Erich Kästner
Fabian: The Story of a Moralist

Valentine Kataev
Time, Forward!

Kharms and Vvedensky
The Man with the Black Coat:
  Russia's Literature of the Absurd

Danilo Kiš
The Encyclopedia of the Dead
Hourglass

Ignacy Krasicki
The Adventures of Mr. Nicholas
  Wisdom

Miroslav Krleza
The Return of Philip Latinowicz

Curzio Malaparte
Kaputt
The Skin

Karin Michaëlis
The Dangerous Age

V. F. Odoevsky
Russian Nights

Andrey Platonov
The Foundation Pit

Bolesław Prus
The Sins of Childhood and Other
  Stories

Valentin Rasputin
Farewell to Matyora

Alain Robbe-Grillet
Snapshots

Arthur Schnitzler
The Road to the Open

Yury Trifonov
Disappearance

Evgeniya Tur
Antonina

Ludvík Vaculík
The Axe

Vladimir Voinovich
The Life and Extraordinary
  Adventures of Private Ivan
  Chonkin
Pretender to the Throne

Stefan Zweig
Beware of Pity